BEWAR
DO NOT REA
BOOK FR
BEGINNING T

Your history class takes a trip to the new wax museum. You and your friends, Liz and Jake, hope the trip will make history less boring. But you have no idea what the Wicked Wax Museum has in store for you!

First, Jake vanishes! Do you and Liz stay in the museum to find him? Or do you leave to get help? If you stay, look out for strange men in doctor's masks. Keep out of the Steaming Room if you can. And beware of wax figures that seem a little too lifelike. Especially that hooded one with the gleaming ax!

If you leave the museum, get ready for a terrifying time. Meet Sybil Wicked and her skull-faced servant, Axel. They've developed a horrible new kind of plastic surgery. Can you and Liz escape before your faces get lifted—right off your bodies?

This scary adventure is all about you. You decide what will happen. And you decide how terrifying the scares will be!

Start on PAGE 1. Then follow the instructions at the bottom of each page. *You* make the choices.

SO TAKE A DEEP BREATH. CROSS YOUR FINGERS. AND TURN TO PAGE 1 TO *GIVE YOURSELF GOOSEBUMPS!*

READER BEWARE —
YOU CHOOSE THE SCARE!

Look for more
GIVE YOURSELF GOOSEBUMPS adventures
from R.L. STINE:

#1 Escape from the Carnival of Horrors
#2 Tick Tock, You're Dead!
#3 Trapped in Bat Wing Hall
#4 The Deadly Experiments of Dr. Eeek
#5 Night in Werewolf Woods
#6 Beware of the Purple Peanut Butter
#7 Under the Magician's Spell
#8 The Curse of the Creeping Coffin
#9 The Knight in Screaming Armor
#10 Diary of a Mad Mummy
#11 Deep in the Jungle of Doom

R.L. STINE
GIVE YOURSELF
Goosebumps®

WELCOME TO THE WICKED WAX MUSEUM

AN
APPLE
PAPERBACK

SCHOLASTIC INC.
New York Toronto London Auckland Sydney

A PARACHUTE PRESS BOOK

ISBN 0-590-84772-4

12 11 10 9 8 7 6 5 4 3 2 1 6 7 8 9/9 0 1/0

Printed in the U.S.A. 40

First Scholastic printing, December 1996

"Cool!" you exclaim to your best friends Liz and Jake. "The field trip to the Wicked Wax Museum is today. I can't believe our class gets to see it the day *before* the grand opening."

"Finally, Mr. Dunning's history class won't be such a bore," Jake adds, flipping his black baseball cap around backwards. "Mr. Dunning. More like Mr. Dull!"

"You said it," Liz giggles. Her red curls bounce when she laughs. "Hey, why is it called the Wicked Wax Museum, anyway?"

"That's the name of the guy who owns it," Jake explains. "Dr. Izzy Wicked. He made all the wax figures."

"Well, according to Mr. Dull," Liz adds, "the museum is supposed to bring history to life for us or something like that."

"Yeah, right." Jake smirks. "And maybe the wax figures will come to life, too."

"Oh, gross!" Liz cries. "You're giving me the creeps, Jake."

"Come on, you two," you say. "The bus is here. Let's be first in line so we can grab the back seats."

Go to PAGE 2.

On the bus, you rush to the back. You and Liz take a two-seater. Jake sits alone across the aisle with his red-sneakered feet on the seat. Now no one else can sit there.

Jake leans back. His chin-length brown hair falls over the top of the seat. "Let's get this crate rolling," he mutters.

"All right, people," Mr. Dunning shouts from the front of the bus. "Thanks to my personal donation to the museum, we get to see the place before it opens to the public tomorrow." The teacher does one last head count. "All right, Sal," he says to the driver. "We're all here. Let's go."

As soon as the bus starts moving, Jake presses his nose and open lips flat against the window for the viewing pleasure of other people on the road. Then he breathes on the window and writes in the steam, HONK IF YOU HATE HISTORY!

"Honk!" you say, laughing.

"Honk, honk!" Liz adds. You and Liz are honking so loud you don't see Mr. Dunning coming down the aisle. He looks mad.

Go to PAGE 3.

"That's enough out of you three! You're always making trouble," the red-faced Mr. Dunning sputters. "If you hate history so much, you can just wait for the rest of us in the lobby."

"Oh brother," you groan. "There goes our fun."

Minutes later, the bus pulls up to a stone building. Mr. Dunning leads the class into the lobby of the Wicked Wax Museum.

A scowling woman in a purple turban and gold bracelets sits inside a ticket booth. "These three students will not be going in," Mr. Dunning tells her. He turns to you, Jake, and Liz and points to a bench by the wall. "Sit there, you little monsters. And you'd better still be sitting there when I come back!"

The class leaves you behind as they enter the Hall of Historical Exhibits. A red door closes after them. Jake manages to sit still for a few minutes. Then he jumps up and says, "I think it's time for us to take a little tour of our own."

Turn to PAGE 75.

4

You know a chance to escape when you see one. You push the door. It swings open!

Immediately the test tubes stop moving. You jump out. The men with the doctor's masks are nowhere in sight. You run back to Liz's tube and unseal her door.

"Thanks!" Liz exclaims as she jumps out.

"Are you alright?" you ask.

"I'm fine," she assures you. "But what about Jake? I can't see him anymore. He disappeared into that opening in the wall!"

Liz is right. Jake's test tube is out of sight.

You run to the opening in the wall. When you peer in, you can't see Jake's tube. But what you do see is so frightening it makes the hair on the back of your neck stand up!

It's the next step. And it couldn't be worse.

A sign at the end of a long tunnel flashes these words: SKIN SCRAPING CENTER.

"They're going to skin Jake alive!" you breathe in horror.

Try your best to save him on PAGE 98!

Nervously, you and Liz step down from the tubes. You glance around for Jake. But you don't see him anywhere.

Where is that voice coming from? you wonder. Then you spot two speakers hanging from wires on the cavelike walls.

"There's no one here," Liz whispers.

A few steps away, you see two bucket seats lined with cushions. Two comfortable chairs just sitting there in the middle of the cave. Without thinking, you and Liz fall into the soft, cushioned seats to collect your thoughts.

"We've lost Jake." You state the obvious. "If only we could find Mr. Dunning and the group!"

"What kind of weird wax museum is this, anyway? There's something terrible happening here," Liz says.

Another recorded message suddenly blares through the cavern: "*For the convenience of other visitors, please keep moving . . .*"

Then the floor beneath your seats starts to move. Just like the test tubes. "Hey!" you shout, trying to get up.

A bar falls down across your lap. Another drops down on Liz.

Wait a minute, you think. You've been in seats like these before. At the amusement park! You must have stumbled onto some sort of wax museum ride. Hope it's a good one!

Hang on as you ride over to PAGE 49.

Liz looks as scared as you feel. "Don't be afraid," the man holding her declares. "The dipping doesn't hurt . . . for long."

"You won't get away with this!" you warn. "Our teacher, Mr. Dunning, is friends with the owner of this place! He made a personal contribution to the museum."

"You're the ones who won't get away," says your captor. "He doesn't know it, but the biggest contribution Mr. Dunning made is you kids! You'll never see your teacher again!"

"That's right," adds Liz's guard. "Dr. Wicked ordered us to make new figures for the unfinished exhibits before the grand opening of the museum tomorrow."

"The press and television newspeople are arriving in two hours!" adds the tall man. "We've got a lot of body dipping to do in a very little time."

"Body dipping?" you screech. "Where's Mr. Dunning? Where's Jake? I demand to see him. *Now!*" And you start to scream.

"Scream all you like, kid," says the short one. "Your friend is being processed. It's done in stages. First the steaming, then the skinning, then the hot wax dipping. It's hard to create exhibits of such horrifying quality, you know."

"But this is supposed to be a history museum!" Liz cries.

Get Liz's answer on PAGE 130.

With your eye on the candle in the window, you start screaming wildly. You fling your arms in the air and flap your hands. You bob your head up and down like a dashboard doll with a loose spring.

"Grab the kid!" the worker shouts at the Strangler.

Liz can't believe her eyes. You've never gone totally berserk before. You wink at her, and then she gets the idea. Now she shrieks wildly, too!

When the attention turns to Liz, you reach for the candle in the window. You wave the flickering flame in the face of the Strangler. Back and forth, closer and closer to his waxy cheeks.

"No!" the man in overalls screams when he sees what you're up to. "Not fire! He'll melt! Take it away!"

It's too late for the Strangler. From beneath the wide brimmed hat, flesh-colored wax drips down in a puddle. The museum worker pushes you aside and tries to glob the hot wax back into place. He looks up at you and snarls, "You'll pay for this. I promise you that!"

Get out of there while you still can. Run to PAGE 109.

You keep running and don't look back. You don't have to see him — now you can hear the Strangler's footsteps behind you. "Hurry, Liz! He's following us!"

You run to the entrance door of the brick apartment building closest to you and try the handle. Locked!

The Strangler is catching up.

You hurry to the next door. Locked!

The Strangler is closing in on you.

Liz trips and stumbles. "My ankle!" she cries, hopping on one foot. "I twisted it!"

The Strangler is gaining on you. You drag Liz to the next door. Locked! All locked. There's only one building left to try. "Liz," you say, pulling her along behind you, "come on, you've got to make it a little farther."

You reach the door of the last building. "There's a candle burning in the window on the top floor," you whisper hoarsely to Liz. "This one's got to open for us!"

Run for PAGE 79.

Liz is right. You've just stepped out of the tornado and into the Skin Scraping Center! It's a laboratory filled with workers in white overalls. They are so busy polishing long steel tables, they don't see you and Liz standing by an electrical control box in the corner.

Jake is here, still strapped onto the rolling stretcher. His mouth and eyes are covered with silver tape. A worker is pushing the stretcher toward a giant steel tumbler. Its beehive shape and the way it turns around on an axis reminds you of the back of a cement truck.

Another worker opens the tumbler door. The inner walls are lined with sandpaper. The worker turns a dial. Inside, a shower of coarse gravel beats against the sandpapered walls. Anything placed in there will be skinned in seconds!

You watch in horror as Jake is wheeled up the ramp and into the skin scraping machine. "Do something!" Liz cries.

Quickly, you open the control box behind you. Inside are two levers. One is marked POWER. The other says POWER LESS.

If you pull the lever marked POWER, *turn to PAGE 48.*

If you pull the lever marked POWER LESS, *turn to PAGE 15.*

"Liz," you say, trying to stay calm. "We've got a problem."

"Problem?" Liz asks. "What problem?" She looks right at you. But she doesn't realize why you're standing so still. "What is it?" she asks, staring at you.

You move your eyes downward. "My hand," you whisper softly. "His hand," you add even more softly.

Liz looks at the Executioner's fingers wrapped tightly around your hand. As she's watching, the Executioner raises his index finger and waves it at Liz.

"He's ALIVE!" she screams.

She lunges forward. Using both hands, she shoves the Executioner backward and throws him completely off balance. The ax goes flying out of his hand.

You scramble over to the ax. It's yours! As the giant creature tries to get up, you raise the ax over your head.

But before you can bring it down again on your black-caped enemy, someone stops you.

"Got you!" says a man's voice.

Turn to PAGE 13 to find out who has you.

"Let's risk the doors," you decide. "You never know what might be lurking under a bed!"

Grabbing Liz's arm, you race to the right-hand purple door and throw it open. It's a closet! And it's full of row after row of identical purple robes.

The footsteps are right outside the room. "No time to waste," Liz whispers. She crowds into the closet with you. Then she pulls the door closed. The only light comes through a large keyhole that's just at eye level.

Even with that little light, you can tell that the closet is deep. In fact, you can't find the back wall at all.

Then the light vanishes. Something is blocking the keyhole. Something that shines faintly.

An eye! Someone is looking through the keyhole!

What should you do now? If you stay very still, maybe the eye won't see you. Or maybe this is the time to find out how far back the closet goes.

You'd better decide fast!

If you stay still, get someone to turn to PAGE 21 for you.

If you explore the closet, feel your way to PAGE 38.

An awful gurgling cry from the doorway behind you makes you both shudder. Jake! There's no time to figure out why the ticket lady is made of wax. Your friend needs your help!

"We'll have to go outside and find the bus driver," you tell Liz. "Come on!"

You step outside the lobby and look for Sal, the bus driver. But he's nowhere in sight. In fact, there isn't a living soul anywhere around you. What are you going to do?

At that moment a long black limousine pulls up next to you. The windows are tinted dark blue. You can't see inside until the passenger-side window slowly glides down.

A uniformed driver leans across the seat. His hat throws a deep shadow that hides his face. But his voice is friendly as he says, "I'm Axel. May I be of some assistance?"

Go to PAGE 69.

Someone yanks the ax out of your hands. You spin around. Your eyes widen in surprise. Two men in doctor's masks and overalls are standing behind you. One is tall and thin. The other one is short and round.

"You're here to finish the exhibits, not to finish them off," sneers the shorter man.

"Thanks to you, we have to start all over with this Executioner exhibit," adds the tall man.

What are they talking about? You and Liz are too stunned to ask. You watch the two men lift up the frozen Executioner and carry him to the conveyor belt. Curls of wax litter the floor.

They lay him down on the belt and watch as he disappears through the red velvet streamers. "Dr. Wicked won't like this. There's no time for do-overs," the short man grumbles.

"As for you two," the other man says, shoving you roughly, "it's time for you to join your friend. He's been waiting for you in the Skin Scraping Center."

"No!" Liz cries. "What have you done to Jake?"

The two men laugh. "Nothing we won't do to you, too," the short one promises.

Turn to PAGE 6.

"We already know where the other end of the chute comes out. So I guess we should investigate the locked door," you say reluctantly.

"If you say so," Liz agrees. "But I'm not going first."

Just what you hoped she wouldn't say. Oh, well.

Clenching your teeth, you brush the sticky spider webs aside until you can see the padlock. You hold it in your palm.

Something brushes the underside of your hand. You look down.

A big, hairy black spider crawls over your palm.

"Yecchh!" You shudder from head to foot.

Then the spider sidesteps to another part of the web. And the rusty padlock crumbles in your hand!

"Nice going!" Liz cheers.

"No problem," you answer modestly.

But the next step isn't so easy. Because you don't know what's on the other side of that door.

Taking a deep breath, you give the door a push. It creaks open. Liz stands back. You step inside and gasp.

You can't believe your eyes!

Turn to PAGE 37.

15

You stare at the levers. Power less really must mean less power, you think. If the machine has less power, maybe it won't start up. "Well," you say to Liz, "here goes nothing."

You pull the lever marked POWER LESS.

Sorry. Bad choice on your part. Power Less simply means *you* are powerless! Powerless to do anything that will save Jake. Or you and Liz.

When you pull the lever, the men in white overalls turn to look at you. They don't run after you. They know you're not going anywhere. You're powerless to move. Jake is on his way into the Skin Scraper now. You glance at Liz and gulp. Your turn in the awful machine is coming soon.

Time to notify your next of skin. Because the end is near. In fact, it's here.

THE END

You push the yellow button. Instantly screams and moans of agony fill your ears. Wall panels open, revealing dioramas on both sides of the hall.

"AAHH!" Liz screams, too. Wax figures from the history of horror pose in gruesome scenes. You're surrounded by villains and monsters! Not the kind of distraction you had in mind.

Count Dracula bares fangs dripping with the blood of the wax victim in his arms. The Creature from the Black Lagoon drags a screaming woman into a steaming swamp.

Mud Monsters, King Jelly Jam, The Mummy — monsters from every GOOSEBUMPS book you've ever read, every movie you've ever seen. They're all here with you in this Exhibit Hall of Horror —

But they're only wax, you tell yourself. Exhibits in the museum. And all that roaring, screaming, and crying? It's being pumped in through speakers. Scary, but fake. Right?

Meanwhile, the Skin Scraping Center sign flashes on and off at the end of the hall — reminding you of the real danger ahead!

Go to PAGE 122.

You come to slowly. You can't remember the last time you felt this lousy! Cautiously, you open one eye.

What you see makes you wish you hadn't. Across from you, eyeballs are staring back at you. They're dangling on long strings, like garlic. Some of them look oddly familiar. . . .

You've got a bad feeling about this. You open your other eye.

Eek!

Take a peek at PAGE 46.

"Jake!" you shout. You lunge to pull him back by his feet. Before you can grab his sneaker, a steel door slams down over the opening. You pull your hands back just in time.

Kneeling on the low platform in front of the conveyor belt, you bang on the steel door. "Jake!" you shout again.

The door slides up. The conveyor belt starts moving forward. You're so startled, you lose your balance. *SPLAT!* You fall flat on your face. You're on the belt! "Liz!" you cry in terror. "Get me off this thing!"

Liz jumps up onto the belt to pull you off.

The belt speeds up! Now both you and Liz are being dragged along through the tunnel.

Up ahead, Jake lies motionless on the moving belt. And at the end of the tunnel a sign flashes on and off. It reads: THIS WAY TO STEAMING ROOM.

Find out more about steaming on PAGE 40.

You decide you'd rather not mess with the blowtorch. "Let's run right at them," you whisper to Liz. "Maybe we can fight our way through."

It's a slim chance. But slim is better than none. "Bombs away!" you shout, and charge at the mass of zombie Sybils.

You smash into Sybil 32. Weird! She's incredibly light — as if she's hollow. She wobbles. Bounces against Sybil 29 and Sybil 44. Falls to the floor. And lies there, helpless.

This is easy! You and Liz plow through the Sybils, pushing and shoving. Right. Left. They topple like bowling pins.

"Hey, I got a spare!" Liz laughs.

"Maybe we should set them up for another frame," you joke.

You notice that Liz is ahead of you. "Slow down," you call.

"I can't!" she yells. "I'm being pulled!"

A second later you're caught in the same powerful suction. Your clothes billow in front of you. It's like being sucked into a vacuum cleaner. You dig in your heels. But you can't stop.

You're dragged toward a lavender screen — and pinned. Helpless! "What's happening?" you shout.

"You'll find out," Axel's voice says. The skull-faced driver steps out from behind some shelves and calls, "Your victims are ready, Miss Sybil!"

Find out what's happening on PAGE 64.

"That's the best idea you've had all day," you tell Liz. Jumping onto the empty rack, you shove off with one foot. "You'll never get us!" you shout to the stranger in the shadows.

WHOOSH! The rack zooms forward. It's just like riding a giant skateboard.

Trouble is, you never did learn to steer your board. . . .

"Look out!" Liz screams as you race toward the far wall. "Go left!"

"I'm trying!" you shout. But it's no use. The rack is totally out of control!

WHAM! It smashes against the wall. You and Liz go flying in different directions. You hit a rack full of wax arms. Then you slide to the floor. Oooh, does your head hurt!

You black out.

Go to PAGE 17.

You freeze.

Bad choice! The door to the closet flies open. A hand reaches in and picks you up by your shirt collar. It's Axel!

"Got you!" the skull-faced driver sneers. He grabs Liz in his other hand. "You didn't think I'd drop you off and not come pick you up, did you? Not when Miss Sybil needs you!"

Axel drags you both over to a lavender chest of drawers. He whips a rope out of a drawer and quickly lashes Liz's arms and legs together.

"Ow," she moans. "This really hurts!"

"Not for long," Axel says with a cackle.

He turns to you and loops the rope around your wrists. Then he pulls it tight. Rough cord bites into your flesh. You're trying to be brave. But you can't help groaning.

Axel is knotting the rope when a heart-rending scream rips the air. You jump. Where did it come from?

"The horror!" a wailing voice cries. "The horror!"

Turn to PAGE 105.

"I'll try the clock," you decide. "It'll connect us with the operator who tells you the time. We can get her to call 911 for us." You push the button with the clock on it.

Instead of hearing a helpful voice on the other end of the line, you hear this recording:

"Good afternoon. At the tone your time will be . . . UP!"

"Uh-oh," Liz says.

The limo surges forward and starts to swerve wildly over the road. At the wheel, Axel cackles like a madman. Oh, no! You're doing 100 miles per hour — straight for the edge of a cliff!

As the limo flies over the edge, you hear:

BEEP!

THE END

"Red!" Liz says. "Like my hair!"

The fortune-teller cackles. Two gold teeth in the front of her mouth glitter in the flashing lights. She looks pleased. "The future it shall be then, my dear."

A sudden wind blows through the hallway. It swirls and whirls around you, whipping Liz's hair into your face.

"What's going on?" you yell.

"What?" Liz yells back. But you can barely hear her! The roaring of the sudden wind fills your ears.

You tuck your head down and lean against the gust. You feel it whip around you like a whirlpool.

It's so strong! You're afraid it's going to rip you apart! It's like a thousand iron hands, tugging at you.

Then . . . you notice that your feet are off the ground.

In an enormous *WHOOSH*, you and Liz are sucked up into the heart of a tornado. You shoot upward. Far below you can see the fortune-teller. She's holding up a sign that reads, "The future is yours."

What can that mean? you think. You're about to find out.

Take a look at your hand. Can you find your lifeline?

If you don't know how to find your lifeline, turn to PAGE 126.

If finding your lifeline is a piece of cake, turn to PAGE 103.

At the very last instant, you manage to duck.

The ax skims over you . . . glances off the wall above Liz, cutting free her tangled curls . . . ricochets back over your head . . . and spins to a quick stop. Right in the waxy back of the evil Executioner.

His mouth falls open in a silent scream. He arches his axed back and stands frozen in that position.

You and Liz gasp in unison.

For the Executioner it's

THE END.

But for you, it's only the beginning of the trouble you're heading for. You hear footsteps behind you.

Hurry! Run to PAGE 91 and HIDE.

You sit in the dark for a moment, not sure what to do.

Then a blood-curdling scream echoes through the darkness! "AAAAHHHHHHHHHHH!" It's Jake. It has to be!

"Let's get out of here," Liz cries. She's frantic.

You hear her squeezing under the lap bar and hopping down onto the track. You do the same. "Wait!" you call.

Then you hear Liz scream.

In the same instant, the floor beneath you gives way and dumps you through a secret opening. "We're falling!" you cry as you drop through darkness.

The fall seems to last forever. Then you see light below. The strong smell of melting candles reaches your nose.

First you smell it. Then you see it. Then you're in it. Bubbling, swirling, boiling wax. You splash right into it.

"Two more," you hear a man's voice say before the hot wax seals your ears forever. "Coat them with wax. Put some new faces on them. And presto — instant wax figures. That one over there can be Dr. Frankenstein." A finger pokes you in the side. "And this one can be the monster."

Well, after all, Mr. Dunning called you a little monster. Guess he was right, in

THE END

The track moves you and Liz toward the opening in the wall.

Then something unexpected happens.

Instead of the track taking you to the Skin Scraping Center straight ahead, your test tube veers off to the left.

Spotlights flicker on along the track. You're not in a tunnel at all now. The test tubes are moving through a well-lit cave with a high ceiling.

Without warning, the test tubes stop moving. The doors swing open slowly.

A recorded voice over a loudspeaker repeats mechanically: "*Watch your step, please, as you are leaving your capsule. Watch your step, please, as you are leaving your capsule. Watch your step, please, as you are leaving your capsule.*"

What's going on? Find out on PAGE 5.

You and Liz leave by a door at the far end of the Deboner Room. It takes you to a long flight of stairs. You go up . . . and up . . . and up. At last you reach the end.

"Whew!" you pant. "We must be really high up now!"

You hurry into a room with two hallways branching off from it. "Maybe one of these halls leads outside," Liz suggests. "I'll check the one on the right. You check the left."

You agree. But as you're moving toward the hall on the left, you notice a round window set into the middle of the floor. Like a porthole. Curious, you kneel down and peer through it.

You're gazing down on what seems to be a scientific laboratory. A black-haired girl in a long, purple robe is examining something in a test tube. Her back is to you. But as you watch, she turns around. You catch a glimpse of her face.

You clap a hand over your mouth before the scream can get out.

Turn to PAGE 52.

You and Liz inspect the Deboner. It's a giant, shallow funnel set into the floor. A cluster of metal arms hangs from the ceiling above it. Some are equipped with drills, saws, and other tools. But most of them end in wicked-looking claws.

CLACK! CLACK! The claws snap menacingly as you draw near.

"Isn't it a clever toy?" someone whispers behind you.

Axel! He sneaked up behind you! You think fast. "Liz, go left!" you order, as you dodge to the right.

Axel lunges after you. And trips over the electrical cord of the Deboner. "Yaah!" he yells as he topples into the funnel.

The Deboner's mechanical arms move in a blur. Before you know it, Axel is hanging in midair, held tightly by dozens of claws. A drill hums toward his heart.

"Help me!" he begs. Tears well up in his eye sockets. "I already lost my face. Don't let me lose all my bones as well. Please!"

You hesitate. You feel kind of sorry for Axel. Even *he* doesn't deserve to be deboned.

On the other hand, if you help him, you might be sorry.

If you think you should help Axel, turn to PAGE 45.

If you don't think you should help him, turn to PAGE 82.

"That tunnel must lead outside. Let's stay on the Dumpster," you say. "We may stink, but we'll be free. Maybe we can even get back to the museum before Mr. Dunning misses us."

The Dumpster rattles into the tunnel. It's pitch-black. But then you see a pinprick of light at the far end. The pinprick grows. And grows. It's daylight!

"Yes!" Liz cheers. "We're out of here!"

What a relief! You're leaning forward eagerly when the Dumpster jerks to a stop. Who-o-oa! You topple forward and land flat on your face. In a mound of moldy tuna casserole.

Big yuck! You sit up, spitting out bits of old fish. You're just in time to see Liz being lifted off the pile by a giant scoop. She screams as she's dumped in a bin on the back of a trash truck.

You're next. The giant scoop sweeps you up. Well, on the bright side, it looks as if you and Liz will go to your doom together. Friends to . . .

THE END

No time to lose. Jake needs your help! You step into the darkness. Liz clutches your arm.

"I — I don't like that motor sound," she stammers.

You don't like it either. But it's too late to turn back now. The heavy red door slams shut behind you. A thick bolt slides into place on its own.

You're locked in!

Slowly, your eyes adjust to the strange red light that fills the room. Then you see what's making the motor sound.

Ahead of you a conveyor belt moves slowly through a velvet-streamered opening into a black tunnel. It reminds you of those luggage carousels at the airport. But there are no suitcases on this conveyor belt. Instead, there's a body. Jake's. And it's moving slowly away from you!

His red sneakers are disappearing into the tunnel.

Then you notice something else. Out of the corner of your eye, you see something move. Across the room. It's only a shadow, but there's definitely something there! What is it?

If you want to find out what's moving through the shadows, turn to PAGE 93.

If you ignore it and just go after Jake, turn to PAGE 18.

Oh, no! The escalator is carrying you up! Back toward Sybil and Axel!

And it's moving very, very quickly!

You squint up through the dimness. Bad news. Axel is standing at the top of the escalator. Light reflects off his bare skull. He's laughing like a maniac.

Well, after all, he *is* a maniac.

"We'll have to run down," you groan.

So you start running again. You're trying to move down faster than the escalator can carry you up.

But no matter how fast or slow you go, the escalator goes exactly the same speed. In the opposite direction.

It's hopeless. "We'll never get to the bottom of this escalator!" Liz announces.

She's right. You're stuck. And you'll never get to . . .

THE END

"You've got to see this," you tell Liz. "It's Sybil Wicked. You won't believe your eyes!"

Liz kneels beside you and gazes through the porthole.

And screams. "What a horrible face!"

At the sound of the scream, Sybil Wicked looks up. She's staring right into your eyes! You're so scared you can't move.

Which is too bad. You'd have been better off running away.

Sybil reaches down and pulls a big purple lever on the floor of the lab. The floor beneath you and Liz caves in.

It's a trap door. And you're falling through it!

THUD! You hit the floor of the lab — face-first. You lie there for a minute, stunned. "Oooooh," you moan.

Then you notice a pair of feet in front of you. Slowly your eyes travel up. Over a purple robe. Past long, black hair.

Your gaze stops at last — on the face of the hideous Sybil Wicked.

Turn to PAGE 62.

"It's so foggy here. Who can tell what this place is?" Liz whispers.

A full moon lights the night sky. A single gas lamp casts weird shadows against the brick walls of the buildings. Liz moves the mist away with her hand and looks around. The gaslight flickers, but nothing else moves. All is quiet. All is still. "It's a city," Liz says softly.

"An empty city, it looks like," you reply a little nervously. "We're the only ones here."

A metal garbage can falls over with a crash and a surprised cat wails in the alley. You turn in the direction of the noise.

And scream. "Liz! Look out! Behind you!"

Liz whirls around and gasps. Uh-oh. You're not the only ones here after all.

Hurry to PAGE 94.

"Never trust anyone named Sybil," you declare.

Liz nods. "Let's let these bodies sleep. We'll find a way out by ourselves."

As quietly as you can, you tiptoe through the aisles. You don't want to wake anybody! It's hard, though. The aisles are very narrow.

You ease around a corner. Oh, no! Your shirt is caught on something. You're stuck! You tug at your shirttail.

CRASH! BANG!

The huge room echoes. It sounds as if you knocked over ten garbage cans! Your heart is in your mouth as you turn around.

A single object is rolling across the floor. Quickly you bend down and snatch it up. Maybe you can simply put it back on its shelf and keep going.

You don't *really* believe it'll be that easy, do you?

When you straighten up, all the Sybils are sitting bolt upright on their metal beds. And they're all pointing at you!

Turn to PAGE 87.

You decide on the blank button. "Here goes nothing," you mutter. Picking up the phone, you press.

BZZZT . . . BZZZT . . . BZZZT . . .

Busy?! " I don't believe this!" you grumble.

But the next time you try, you hear a click. Then a recorded voice comes over the line.

"I'm sorry. Your call cannot go through . . . but YOU can!"

The limo screeches to a halt. In the mirror, you catch a glimpse of Axel's face. It's furious! As furious as a bare skull can look, that is.

The floor of the limousine drops out. A trap door! Your seat belt flies open. Next thing you know, you and Liz are shooting down a long, sloping tunnel.

Drop down to PAGE 66.

"Break the glass!" Liz shouts.

"Don't!" Sybil screeches.

"DO IT!" Liz commands.

You're not arguing. You're too busy pulling a wax leg off the rack in front of you. You hold it by the foot and swing it like a baseball bat against the glass box.

CRASH! Bits of glass shower down on the floor. A hidden door slides open in the wall, and a deafening alarm goes off.

The whole room vibrates and hums from the sound waves. It's like an earthquake! The lights sway, casting wild shadows. Rows of legs, arms, lips, and eyeballs dance on the racks. They slap, kick, and pummel Sybil and Axel.

You decide to take this opportunity to say good-bye. "Let's go, Liz!" you shout.

"Stop them!" Sybil commands. She's buried under a mound of mixed lips and ears. "They're getting away!"

"This way!" you shout to Liz, and dash out the exit.

Head for PAGE 83.

"What is it?" Liz cries, moving up behind you. Then she sees what you see. "Oh, wow!" she mutters. "Too strange!"

You're in someone's bedroom. Everything is purple. The walls. The furniture. The bedspread is lavender. Two doors in the far wall are painted dark plum. But it's not the purple that's getting to you. It's not the fact that there are no windows, either. It's what's on the walls.

Dozens of giant, blown-up photos — and they're all of your face and Liz's!

You and Liz walk slowly around the room, studying the pictures. They're all marked up. Your nose, your eyes, your mouth are covered with circles, arrows, and measurements. Someone has penciled notes next to them. "Excellent nostrils." "Correct lower lip. Upper lip good." "Adjust eye color."

Liz calls you from across the room. "You've got to see this," she says. "It gets worse!"

Go to PAGE 95.

How can you stay perfectly still when you're shaking like a blob of Jell-O? You decide to look for another way out.

Shoving Liz ahead of you, you push through the purple robes. Behind you, the closet door flies open. A familiar voice calls out, "Peekaboo, I see you. And I'm coming to get you!"

It's Axel! "Hurry," you mutter.

"Hey!" Liz exclaims. "There's something here. It's a —"

The rest of her words are cut off. You charge toward the back of the closet, batting hanging robes out of your way. "Liz!" you shout. "Where are you?"

Then you smash into a flat, smooth surface. It feels like glass. And it's moving. You're in a revolving door!

You spin through the revolving door and stumble out the other side. Ahead of you stretches a long room. But you only get a glimpse of it. Because there's nothing under your feet. You're falling!

Plunge to PAGE 97.

BZZZZZ! The buzzing sound is suddenly much louder.

You're in a room so big you can't even tell where it ends. All you can see is aisle after aisle of metal shelves. They look like bookshelves. But these shelves are stacked with . . . bodies!

Bodies in long, purple robes. They seem to be sleeping. That's what the buzzing noise is. They're snoring!

Fascinated, you step closer and peer at one. Its skin has a strange, waxy glow. On its sleeve is embroidered SYBIL 67. The one on the shelf above it is labeled SYBIL 82. Creepy!

Each face is slightly different from the others. One has a big nose. Another has no eyebrows. One even has no upper lip.

"These must have something to do with those experiments we were told about," Liz whispers. "I bet Sybil Wicked used these people somehow in her face-replacement experiments."

That gives you an idea. "So maybe all these people are mad at Sybil," you say. "Maybe if we wake them up, they'll help us get out of here."

"Maybe," Liz says. "Or maybe they'll turn us in!"

What should you do? Better make up your mind!

If you try to wake the sleeping Sybils, turn to PAGE 85.

If you decide not to, turn to PAGE 34.

"Steaming Room?" you ask Liz. "What do you suppose that is?"

Liz only shakes her head. And the conveyor belt comes to a sudden stop.

You squint, trying to peer ahead in the darkness. You're about to call out Jake's name when you hear voices.

"Let's get him off this belt," says one man.

"Dr. Wicked wants this one steamed right away. We'll do him first and then get the others," says a second man.

"Steamed?" you gasp.

"And we must be the 'others'!" Liz cries.

"Shhh! Listen!" you say as the voices begin to argue.

"Maybe we should skip the steaming," one man says. "If Dr. Wicked wants us to be finished in time for the opening tomorrow, we might just have to go on to the next step."

"No way!" says the other man. "You know we can't skip any steps. If the steaming is skipped, nothing goes right."

"Okay, okay. Let's just get this kid into the tube."

You and Liz glance at each other in horror. Jake's always had a knack for getting into trouble, but this time he's out of his league!

Turn to PAGE 59.

You jump. Who yelled?

When you look the other way down the hall, your heart sinks. Standing at the far end is Axel. Even at this distance, his fleshless face gives you shivers. Exactly what happened to him? you wonder. But there isn't time to think about that right now. Because Axel is moving toward you. Fast.

You try to keep calm. "Maybe we should run," you tell Liz.

She doesn't answer. That's when you realize she's already halfway down the hall.

"Wait for me!" you yell, and sprint after her.

You catch up to Liz at the end of the hall. "There's no way out," she pants. "Let's see what's behind one of these doors."

She throws open a door and you dash through. Then you slow down to look around. Where *are* you?

This room looks like the kitchen of a fancy restaurant. It's full of gleaming, stainless-steel machines. There's one that looks like a giant mixer, and another with dozens of sharp blades. It's labeled PEELER.

But the one that really gives you chills is the DEBONER.

Turn to PAGE 28.

The *WHACK* of the ax on the chopping block is followed by a *THUD!* The severed head rolls and lands at your feet.

"AHHHHH!" you scream. Two glassy eyes are staring up at you.

But wait! Those aren't Jake's eyes at all!

"They're marbles!" you exclaim to Liz. "This is just a wax figure. It's part of the exhibit. It doesn't even look like Jake! Except for the hair."

"Ha!" Liz laughs nervously. "I wasn't fooled for one minute. Were you?" She looks at the headless wax figure and shudders.

"I wasn't scared," you reply, trying to sound braver than you feel. To prove it, you reach up and tweak the Executioner's waxy nose. "It's all fake, see?"

"Yeah," Liz says, giving the towering figure's cheek a pinch. "Just fake!"

You're not so sure anymore, though. You don't want to scare Liz or anything, but when you touched his nose you felt . . . what was it . . . ? Breath?

Yes. Warm breath. Coming from the Executioner.

But that's impossible! Or is it?

Take a deep breath yourself and turn to PAGE 86.

You turn back and come face-to-face with the man in overalls. He's furious and ready for revenge. His arms are full of what's left of the Strangler. Pieces of his evil face, loose fingers, and masses of melted wax overflow from the museum worker's cradled arms.

"You can't get away with this!" he shouts. "The Strangler won't allow you to escape so easily." He hurls huge globs of wax at you and Liz.

You try to run but your feet get stuck in the sticky piles of the Strangler's waxy remains. The angry worker hurls more and more of the melting wax. *SMACK! THWACK! THWONK!* Soon you're both buried in the waxy remains of the Strangler.

The wax hardens. You can't move. Both of you stand stiff and still. The museum worker examines the results of his wax attack. "Yes," he snarls gleefully. "Nobody beats the Strangler. He's got his hands all over you. And I mean *all* over you."

THE END

You won't show Sybil Wicked's face to Liz, you decide. She'll just get creeped out.

"I'm not looking at anything," you answer quickly. "Come on, let's investigate this left-hand hall." Taking Liz's arm, you pull her past the porthole and down the short hallway.

At the end is a purple velvet curtain. Behind it, you can hear a low, steady buzzing noise. A sign pinned to the heavy cloth says DO NOT DISTURB.

Would it be rude to ignore the sign? "My parents always taught me —" you begin to say.

Then you hear voices behind you. You recognize one as Axel's. The other is a girl's voice. It's saying:

"My victims must be here somewhere. We must find them!"

This is no time to worry about rudeness! You and Liz quickly duck under the purple curtain.

Turn to PAGE 39.

"I think we should help Axel," you whisper to Liz.

She makes a face. "Are you kidding? He kidnapped us and brought us to this weird place. Who knows what horrible things he was going to do with us? And now you want to help him? What if he comes after us again?"

She has a point. Maybe you should think again.

Still want to help Axel? Okay, turn to PAGE 136.

Changed your mind? Go to PAGE 82.

46

Your two eyes are staring into each other — from about ten feet apart!

You scream.

Your voice comes from all the way across the room!

Both your eyes swivel wildly. Now you can see other bits of you, hanging on nearby racks. There's your right arm . . . and your left foot . . . and that ear over there is Liz's! You recognize her gold earring!

"Too bad they got so banged up. Now I'll have to find some new victims for the Face Lifter. Oh, well, at least we saved some of their body parts for the other experiments," a voice says. You recognize it as Axel's. But you can't tell where it's coming from, because you don't know where your ears are.

You wonder what "other experiments" are in store for you. You're sure you'll find out soon. Anyway, there's nothing you can do now. There's no point in getting all broken up about it!

THE END

You try to save oxygen in this glass prison by standing perfectly still. Apparently, Liz has the same idea. She breathes slowly inside her tube. You can't see Jake at all. His tube is filled with a cloud of white steam.

Your mind works overtime. What's this all about? Those two men talked about getting you ready for Dr. Wicked. They said this steaming was just the first step. First step of what? You're not sure you want to know. You'd rather just get out alive!

Steam whooshes in through a hose in the top of the test tube. You brace yourself for the pain. . . .

But it never comes! Instead, your pores open as the steam gives your skin a deep cleansing. It's hot, but not so hot you can't stand it.

Then, as suddenly as the steam appeared, it clears. You see you're moving again. The test tubes are lined up along a rolling track. Jake's tube is far ahead of you, rattling as it goes.

Behind you, Liz looks as surprised as you that it's over. You raise your hand to the glass to wave at her.

As you do, you bump the latch on the glass door — and it wiggles loose!

Turn to PAGE 4.

You stare at the lever marked POWER. What will happen if you pull it? you wonder.

"Do it," Liz whispers. "Pull the lever."

You look over at the skin scraping machine, then back at the lever. The door of the steel tumbler is closed. Jake's muffled cries can be heard from inside.

The man in white overalls reaches for the dial to start the machine. His hand is almost on it. You pull the POWER lever.

KABOOM! Sparks fly from the control box and from the dials on the skin scraping machine. All the circuits are shorting out. The man in overalls pulls his hand back and covers his face just before the second *KABOOM* blasts open the door.

The whole laboratory is shaking. You and Liz hold onto each other and watch as Jake's stretcher rolls out of the tumbler and down the ramp. Jake is still strapped in. His eyes and mouth are still taped shut. He can't see what you see.

The chair is rolling wildly out of control. "Oh, no!" cries Liz. "He's heading right for the . . ."

"Wax Dipping Laboratory!" you cry out together!

Try to catch up with Jake on PAGE 92.

The seats move forward into yet another dark tunnel. It's so dark you can't even see your hand in front of your face.

Then your seat swivels abruptly and the lights come up.

Before you is a wax diorama. It shows a stone-walled room filled with weird, old-fashioned science equipment. In the middle of the floor is a doctor's examining table. You recognize the setting — you've seen the movie at least five times.

It's a scene from *Frankenstein*!

But there's something wrong. A wax statue of Igor, the creepy assistant, stands with his hand on the power switch. His mouth is open as if he's talking to someone. Except that there's no one else there. What's more, the examining table is empty.

Where's Dr. Frankenstein?

And where's the monster?

Weird! You know the museum is set to open tomorrow. So where are the missing statues? Maybe you should investigate.

Liz has a different plan in mind.

Turn to PAGE 131.

You glance back over your shoulder to see if the Strangler is following you. "Hey!" you exclaim with relief. You stop running and stare back in amazement. "He isn't moving!"

From where you're standing it's obvious that the Strangler isn't as scary as you thought he was.

"Is he made out of wax?" Liz asks breathlessly.

"Yeah! That's what I think," you declare. "Boy, are we stupid. Let's go back and take a closer look."

You run back down the block to where the figure still stands with his hands stretched out, ready to strangle his next victim.

Ah-ha! Just as you thought. "He's wax, all right," you laugh. "This whole setup is just another scene."

Liz stops before she gets too close. "Are you sure he's wax?" she asks nervously. "Are you absolutely sure?"

Go to PAGE 113.

After a second, the bucket seats start up again. You turn a corner. There's light up ahead.

A recorded voice says, "We hope you've enjoyed the show. Please watch your step as you leave the ride." The bars lift from your laps and you step out.

You're in a little room with mirrors on the pale green walls. On one wall there's an open door. A sign above it says WELCOME TO THE "RIVER OF WAX" MAZE. PROCEED AT YOUR OWN RISK.

Beyond it, a narrow path is bordered by clear glass ditches. What looks like hot wax flows through the ditches — popping and bubbling as it goes. Now you see why it's risky to enter this maze. You wouldn't want to slip and fall into the wax!

Liz starts to say something, but you cut her off. "Shhhh!" you caution. "I think I hear something. . . ."

Sure enough, barely audible above the gurgle and pop of the wax, you hear voices. You can't make out what they're talking about, but you know who they are. You'd know those voices anywhere. How could you forget them?

"It's them!" you whisper to Liz. "The guys with the doctor's masks. We must be close to Jake! Come on!"

You have no choice but to tackle the maze on PAGE 96. Good luck!

The face of the girl in the lab is a real horror!

It looks as if it's been stitched together from many different faces. Seams crisscross her cheeks. The skin is all different colors. A tuft of red hair grows right out of the middle of her forehead. One eye is blue. The other is brown. The brown eye is bigger than the blue eye. And it's two inches higher up on her face!

Then you realize who you're staring at. It can only be Sybil Wicked.

"This is a dead end," Liz complains as she emerges from the right-hand hallway. "How about the other — hey! What are you looking at?"

You hesitate. Sybil's face is really scary, you think. Should you let Liz see it? Or should you spare her some nightmares?

If you decide to show her, turn to PAGE 32.
If you decide to spare her, turn to PAGE 44.

A glare of yellow light blinds you. It's as if someone just turned on the sun! You shade your eyes until they adjust.

You jump back. You're staring at your own face! A clone? No. You're looking in a mirror. The room is lined with them. Pocket mirrors. Hand mirrors. Rear-view mirrors. Bathroom mirrors. They cover the walls. The door. The ceiling. Even the floor!

One bare light bulb hangs from a cord in the middle of the room. The light from that bulb bounces back and forth from mirror to mirror. Multiplying. That's why the light is so strong.

And getting stronger . . .

"Oh, no!" Liz moans. "The bulb is glowing brighter!"

It's already too bright. And hot. And now there's a sizzling sound. You squint at your reflection. Is that smoke coming out of your ears?

The next thing you hear is Liz. Screaming. "My face!" she cries. "It's melting!"

"I told you you'd be sorry!" Axel yells through the door.

You know what? For once, you wish you'd listened to him. But it's too late now. Because you're frying up faster than you can say . . .

THE END

"I can't help you escape," Axel tells you. "But I can give you something that might help you later on."

He takes a round mirror from his jacket pocket. "Keep this," he says, handing it to you. "It might come in handy."

"What for?" Liz asks. "Why would we need a mirror?"

"I can't tell you," Axel says.

"Can you at least tell us why we're here?" you ask.

Axel sighs. "My boss is Sybil Wicked," he says. "She's a scientist like her father, Dr. Izzy Wicked. Three years ago Miss Sybil was in a fire. Everyone thinks she died, but she didn't. She lived — but her face was horribly burned. Since then she's been living in secret, working on a way to make a new face for herself. But she needs someone else's face to do it."

You shudder. "You mean she wants to — to steal our faces? Is that what happened to you, Axel?"

Axel nods. "An early experiment," he explains. "It didn't work. But Miss Sybil kept me as her servant."

What a gruesome story! You can't let it happen to you!

"Now go," Axel tells you and Liz. "I'll count to a thousand before I come after you again. Good luck!"

You tiptoe away as he starts to count.

Sneak to PAGE 27.

You push the green button. The ceiling above you opens up. A large pair of tongs reaches down and lifts you and Liz up through the opening in the ceiling.

As you rise, you see the floor below speeding downward and away from you. In fact, you realize you're not moving up at all. The tongs are holding you in place while all that is below you sinks farther and farther away!

"Are they just going to keep us hanging here?" you wonder aloud.

You spoke too soon. A veil of mist gathers at your feet. Your feeling of dangling in midair disappears. Solid ground is under your feet again. You peer down and see that you're standing on a sidewalk.

The tongs release you and vanish. When you glance up to see what happened to them, you see a row of small apartment buildings. "Hey, what is this place?" you say.

Turn to PAGE 33.

"Yuck! Total gross-out!" you declare.

You're looking at Sybil Wicked's true face. But it isn't really a face. It's a head-shaped nest of purple slime. Worms and maggots slither in and out of its eye sockets. A beetle creeps along its cheek. Slimy goo drips from its chin onto the floor.

"You're not Dr. Wicked's daughter!" you cry. "You're not even human!"

"Correct!" the Sybil-monster agrees. "I am the doctor's most beautiful living wax creation. Or I was. Until the fire made me mutate into . . . this. A thing so hideous I don't even dare to look at myself in the mirror."

The Sybil-monster starts to weep as she comes toward you. You can't blame her. You'd even feel sorry for her. That is, if she wasn't about to seize you and steal your face!

Then something she said gives you an idea. If only you had a mirror handy!

If you picked up a MIRROR somewhere in this adventure, go to PAGE 60.

If you didn't, go to PAGE 58.

The hand belongs to Sybil Wicked. You were wrong. You didn't get her after all. She got you. And she's mad.

"You've made a lot of trouble for me," she snarls. "Now I'm going to make some for you."

You know she's not kidding. You struggle. But her grip is too strong to break.

"Let me go!" you hear Liz yelling. Out of the corner of your eye, you see her. She's trying to break away from Sybil's mad servant, Axel. But she's not having any luck.

Sybil and Axel drag you and Liz to the other end of the huge room. There they stand you with your backs against a lavender screen. "Turn on the Suction Screen, Axel," Sybil orders.

Axel flips a giant purple switch. An instant later, you and Liz are sucked backward and pinned against the screen. You pull with all your might. But you can't move your arms and legs.

Go to PAGE 64.

You search your pockets frantically. But it's no use. You never carry a mirror.

The Sybil-monster grabs you. She holds you with one hand. With the other, she wheels the Face Lifter forward.

"Your face is mine," she croons. "Relax. Don't fight it."

Her putrid flesh is so horrifying that you can't even struggle. You hang limp in her grasp, staring helplessly.

The mechanical arms of the Face Lifter reach toward you. Tiny drills whirl. Pincers snap. Scalpels slice.

You can't bear to watch anymore. You shut your eyes.

Turn to PAGE 110.

"We've got to see what they're doing!" you whisper.

You and Liz tiptoe along the conveyor belt. Finally you can see the room at the end of the tunnel. Two men are lifting Jake off the conveyor belt. His body hangs limp. You watch in terror as they load him into a tall glass tube and shut the door.

The room is filled with these human-sized tubes. They look like big test tubes, but they have doors. Each tube also has a clear hose sticking out of the top, connecting it to a big pipe on the ceiling. And Jake is inside one of them!

"How can we get him out of there?" Liz whispers.

Before you can answer, the conveyor belt starts up again with a jolt. You and Liz are knocked off your feet and carried down the tunnel . . . toward the test tube room!

Then you notice that the air around you is getting damp and heavy. And you're feeling sleepy. Very sleepy!

You spot purple smoke hissing from under the conveyor belt. Sleeping gas! It registers in your brain, but your body is now helpless to do anything about it! It's all you can do to rock your head to the side so you can see where you're going.

No surprise there. You and Liz are headed straight into the waiting hands of two men in gloves and doctor's masks!

Turn to PAGE 133 to see what happens next!

60

You slap your pockets frantically. Axel gave you a mirror after you rescued him from the Deboner. What did you do with it?

The Sybil-monster's disgusting, rotting breath is right in your face. If she gets any closer the worms from her face will crawl over to yours. Where *is* that mirror?

There! You find the small disk in your back pocket. Pulling it out, you thrust it in the Sybil-monster's face.

"The horror!" she cries as she sees her own reflection. "The horror! The horror!"

She said she couldn't bear to look at herself in a mirror. Will it stop her?

It does — and more! The Sybil-monster begins to melt into a pool of purple liquid. The nest of creepy-crawlies spreads out over the puddle and begins to slurp it up. Soon there'll be nothing left of Sybil Wicked.

Voices approach. It's Liz — with a mob of reporters! "They're here for Sybil's press conference," she explains.

Flashbulbs go off all around you. Reporters buzz with questions. The press has arrived just in time to catch Sybil's final moments on film. "What a story!" one of them cries.

It sure is. And you and Liz are the real heroes, in . . .

THE END

"Down," you decide. "Let's go!"

You and Liz bound down the escalator steps two at a time. You're running . . . running . . . running. . . .

Finally you slow to a walk. You're exhausted!

"Where does this thing end?" Liz grumbles. "I've never been on such a long escalator."

You've been wondering about something else. "Does it seem to you like this thing *is* slowing down?" you ask.

Soon there's no question. The escalator *is* slowing down.

Then it stops completely.

Then it starts moving again. In the other direction!

Turn to PAGE 31.

Before you can react, Sybil hauls you up and ties you to a chair. Liz is already tied to another one next to you. Your nose throbs and your lip feels like it might be split. Liz has a black eye.

Sybil paces, grumbling to herself. "These faces are ruined!" she whines. "Flattened! Bent! Swollen! I can't use them now. They look as bad as the one I already have!"

"Too bad," you remark. "I guess that means you'll have to let us go, doesn't it?"

Sybil laughs. "Hah! I can't let you go now. You could get me in trouble! No, I think I'll keep you for my other experiments."

"Wh-what other experiments?" Liz stammers.

"You'll find out soon enough," Sybil says, smirking.

Not soon enough, as far as you're concerned. Axel carts you away to a giant hamster cage. The only thing there is to do there is run on a giant exercise wheel. Which gets really boring, really fast. After a week, you're just wishing for . . .

THE END

You're left-handed? Congratulations! The Executioner is holding your right arm. But your strongest arm is free.

Great gobs of wax hang in hideous shreds from the Executioner's face, arms, and neck. He's still peeling.

Underneath the wax, patches of burned and raw flesh ooze! He's half flesh, half wax. But he's *all* bad!

His blade is aimed at your neck. You reach your left hand up and grab the handle of the ax.

The Executioner pulls it back. You grit your teeth and yank as hard as you can. His waxy hands can't hold on. He lets go!

But his sudden loss of grip surprises you. You go flying backwards. And so does the ax!

You watch in horror as the blade comes spinning through the air. Right toward your face!

Turn to PAGE 24.

"Fetch the Face Lifter!" Sybil commands. "And hurry! It's almost time for my press conference!"

Axel disappears down the aisles of shelves. A moment later he returns. He's pushing a shiny stainless steel machine in front of him. It looks like an octopus, with lots of metal arms that wave in the air. Each arm is tipped with a different lethal-looking instrument.

"Excellent," Sybil gloats. She and Axel bend over the machine, making last-minute adjustments.

"There's the Chin Skinner," Liz moans. "And that one must be the Eye Popper. And —"

"Shut up," you beg. You don't want to hear it! Without thinking, you slide away from Liz. That's when you realize you might have a chance after all. Because you *can* move — sideways! You can slide along the Suction Screen!

You make sure that Axel and Sybil are still busy with the Face Lifter. Then you start slithering. It's hard work, but you slide all the way to the giant purple switch. If you can only move your hand enough to flip it to OFF . . .

Flip to PAGE 117.

"Mr. Dunning!" you, Liz, and Jake all cry at once. "What are you doing here?"

"Good question," Mr. Dunning says angrily. "I might ask you the same thing! I thought I told you to wait in the lobby!"

"Ah . . . well . . . we . . . uh . . ." Jake stammers.

"Never mind that now. I'll deal with you three later. Maybe missing this wonderful trip was punishment enough. We saw everything there was to see and even met the owner of the museum himself, Dr. Wicked. Haven't seen him lately, though. Anyway, you three really missed out on a lot. I hope you've learned a lesson after this experience."

"Oh, we sure have, Mr. Dunning," you say. "We definitely, positively, sure have!"

THE END

"Whoa!" you cry. You're on a metal slide, bouncing off stone walls. Down, down, down you go. Finally you land with a *THUD*.

"Wh-where are we?" Liz stammers as she picks herself up.

You gaze around. You're in a windowless little room that looks like a dungeon cell. Greenish water oozes down slimy stone walls and makes puddles at the bottom.

In one corner, there's a wooden door. It's held closed by a rusted chain and a big padlock. The door, chain, and lock are thickly covered with spider webs. Ugh! You shudder. Spiders give you the creeps!

"I don't know where we are," you reply, brushing yourself off. "But I know we've got to get out of here before that weirdo Axel finds us."

"Yeah," Liz agrees. "And if we don't get back to the wax museum before Mr. Dunning misses us, we've had it!"

You don't really want to go through the spider webs to the door. You gaze up at the chute that dumped you here. You might be able to climb back up. But will the skull-faced Axel be waiting for you?

If you try the locked door, turn to PAGE 14.
If you try to climb the chute, turn to PAGE 114.

"Don't look down!" you warn Liz. It's too late. She's already seen what you've seen. She knows hot wax when she smells it and she's panicked!

"I'm not waiting around to be dropped into that!" Liz says, batting her arms against the sides of the wind funnel.

Suddenly Liz's arms break through the solid wall of wind. Right before your eyes, she is sucked out of the funnel!

"Liz!" you shout. Seconds later, her arm reaches in from outside, grabs your arm, and yanks you out, too!

"Ugh!" you say, trying to catch your breath. "My stomach feels like it exploded! I didn't think we were going to make it for a minute there."

"Uh-oh," Liz gulps as she looks around. "I have a feeling we're not out of danger yet. . . ."

Turn to PAGE 9.

A blowtorch! "Excellent!" you cry, and turn on the gas.

WHOOSH! A blue flame shoots out. You aim the fire at the nearest zombie Sybil — number 68. "Back off!" you command.

The Sybils gasp and step back. But Sybil 68 is too close to the flame. Her face turns shiny. Then her mouth starts to sag.

"She's melting," Liz gasps. "Hey! She's made of wax!"

Liz is right! And you're saved!

Waving the torch, you advance on the wax Sybils. "Take that, candleheads!" you shout. Wax figures melt like ice cream on a hot day. Then you hear a female voice. Shrieking.

"My models! My beautiful wax me's! Ruined!"

It's the real Sybil. She's there, too. But you have no idea which one she is! There's only one way to handle this. Shutting your eyes, you spray fire until the blowtorch is empty.

Silence. You open your eyes. Purple wax coats the floor as far as you can see. And there's no sign of the real Sybil.

You must have torched her. "Wow!" you say. "What a —"

Your sentence ends in a gurgle. Because a hand shoots out from behind a lump of wax and grabs your throat.

Go to PAGE 57.

"Help!" Liz cries. "Our friend is trapped in the museum and we can't find anyone to help us rescue him!"

"Calm down," Axel says. "There's a phone in the backseat. Get in! You can call for help."

The limo's back door opens. You spot the phone. But that's not all you see. This car is equipped with the works! There's a television, a refrigerator filled with sodas and snacks, a CD player, and every CD anyone could want.

"Wow! This car is loaded!" you declare.

The driver laughs. "That's right. Hop in and help yourselves to a soda! Put on some music!"

Your parents always told you never to get into a stranger's car. On the other hand, you do need to call for help — and a cold soda sure would taste good!

What should you do?

If you decide to get into the limo, go to PAGE 118.

If you decide you'd better not, go to PAGE 135.

70

You're right-handed? Really? Too bad. The Executioner grabbed your right hand. So you can fight back only with your weaker left one.

His ax blade is raised. You reach up your left hand to hold it back. It's no use. You can't win against his strength. The blade is sinking!

It's getting closer. And closer. It's only an inch away! You strain against it with all your might.

Right then, a blast of icy air comes down through one of the ceiling vents.

In less than a second, both you and the Executioner are frozen stiff. He stands poised with his ax ready to chop. Where are you? You're frozen in position directly under the blade!

"Perfect!" you hear a man's voice say. "My Executioner has his victim, and I have another exhibit ready for the opening tomorrow." He laughs a wicked laugh and adds, "They don't called me Dr. Wicked for nothing!"

It's the evil owner of the museum himself — Dr. Izzy Wicked.

Iz-zy Wicked?

Yes, he is!

THE END

"Go for a thin rope!" you call out to Liz. You both grab hold of the thinner ropes. Before you can start climbing, the ropes automatically lift you up. They swing you through the rows and rows of wax-dipped figures.

Higher and higher you go until you stop directly over the vats of bubbling wax.

"Cut them loose!" Dr. Wicked cries from his platform.

A worker holds an oversized pair of hedge cutters. On the order from Dr. Wicked, he cuts the thin ropes. You and Liz drop to the vats below.

The next sounds you hear are voices of children on a field trip to the Wicked Wax Museum. "Wow! Check this scene out!" one kid says. "It's kids like us getting dipped in hot wax!"

So that's it, you think to yourself. This is the scene you and Liz were meant to be in all along. You're just two kids being dipped in vats of hot wax in a wax museum. At least your audience is enjoying the show. As for you, your performance has come to . . .

THE END

You decide to try the laughing jester button. "This one looks sort of friendly," you declare. Picking up the phone, you push the button.

BZZT . . . BZZT . . . BZZT . . . BZZT . . .

Busy.

"You mean they don't have call waiting?" Liz grumbles.

You try again.

BZZT . . . BZZT . . . BZZT . . . BZZT . . .

Still busy.

Want to try again? Or would you rather try one of the other phone buttons?

To try the laughing jester again, turn to PAGE 108.

To try the button with the clock, turn to PAGE 22.

To try the blank button, turn to PAGE 35.

"I'd rather not find out," Liz declares. "We've got to get out of here! Come on, let's try those doors."

"Wait a second," you call. You've spotted a blueprint tacked to the wall by the bed. You cross the room for a closer look. Liz is right behind you.

Detailed drawings show a machine that looks like a steel octopus. Eight robotic arms reach out from a round, stainless steel cylinder. Each arm has a different function and is labeled clearly: FACE PEELER, EYE POPPER, LIP RIPPER, EAR ERASER, NOSE NIPPER, CHIN SKINNER, BONE BREAKER, SKIN SCALER.

The machine is labeled: THE FACE LIFTER.

"Oh, gross!" Liz exclaims. "It lifts the features right off your face! Do you think that's what happened to Axel?"

Before you can answer, you hear footsteps outside the room. It's hard to tell which direction they're coming from. You need to hide. But should you risk going through one of the doors and maybe running into someone? Or should you dive under the bed?

If you go for one of the doors, turn to PAGE 11.
If you dive under the bed, turn to PAGE 90.

"We already know the door on the right is just a closet," you declare. "We'll check out the other one."

You stick your head cautiously through the left-hand doorway. Beyond it is a short hall with two more doors. The first one is painted purple. You can hear a voice behind that one. Axel's voice.

"Not that way," Liz whispers.

Your heart pounds as you tiptoe past the first door. But no one comes out. No one grabs you.

You put your hand on the knob of the second door. This door is bright yellow. You wonder why it isn't purple like the rest.

Then a sudden noise behind you almost makes your heart stop!

Turn to page 112.

"Jake! Don't!" you whisper loudly as he disappears through the red door. You glance at the ticket lady. She's busy with something in the booth. "Jake!" you call again. "We're in enough trouble already!"

You jump up from the bench and try to grab the door before it closes. Too late! The red door slams in your face.

"Hey! Open up!" You hear Jake yelling through the door. He rattles the knob. "Help!" he cries.

Liz leaps up to help you push the door open. It won't budge.

"Ha, ha, funny. Stop kidding around, Jake!" she scolds.

"Help!" Jake screams again. He really does sound scared.

Then you hear a whir, like a motor starting up. The click of gears mingles with Jake's cries. "Jake!" you shout.

There's no answer. You press your ear against the door and listen. "I think something is *really* wrong," you whisper to Liz. "His cries are getting farther away. We have to get in!"

You shake the door handle and give one last push. Suddenly the door opens easily. Darkness greets you both. Darkness and the loud whirring of a motor. No sign of Jake.

If you go in after Jake, turn to PAGE 30.

If you decide to get help first, go to PAGE 111. But HURRY!

"I think we should get out of the Dumpster. It might be going to an incinerator," you point out. "We'll find another way out of this crazy place."

"Right," Liz agrees. "Let's go!"

The two of you scramble over the side of the big Dumpster and jump down to the floor. Not a moment too soon! The Dumpster plunges into the tunnel and is swallowed by the darkness.

You're in what looks like a basement. It's huge and dimly lit. A set of rails snakes past your feet — the tracks the Dumpster moves on. "Let's follow these back and see where they start," Liz suggests.

It's a good idea. You trace the tracks backward until they disappear into another dark tunnel. You don't want to follow them in there. Instead you climb the seven steps next to them.

At the top of the steps is an arched doorway. Cautiously you stick your head through. You're looking down a long hall lined with purple doors.

"Aha!" yells a voice behind you. "There you are!"

Hurry to PAGE 41.

"I told those kids to wait in the lobby!" the voice repeats. "Now they're holding up the whole group. I told those kids to wait in the lobby! Now they're holding up the whole group!"

There, on a closet shelf, sits a tape recorder. It's playing a tape labeled DUNNING AUDIO in black magic marker. The door slams behind you. And you hear the lock turn.

"It's only a tape recording of Mr. Dunning's voice," you whisper. You're too stunned to scream.

Liz starts pounding on the door, but it's no use. No one's going to let you out.

You're trapped in here with the voice of Mr. Dunning playing endlessly. *"I told those kids to wait in the lobby! Now they're holding up the whole group!"*

The Executioner was bad, but this is horrible! What could be worse than listening to Mr. Dunning's dull voice forever? Whoever said history never repeats itself?

Looks as if you're doomed to be bored to death in . . .

THE END

The wax on the hand of the Executioner peels away easily. You flick a soft lump of the stuff off your finger and scratch some more.

This time you scrape a patch on his arm. You dig deeper with your nail. Under the cool layers of wax you feel a warm spot. You squint your eyes and look closer. Is it only flesh-colored wax?

Or is it really flesh?

Turn to PAGE 132.

You turn the handle. The door is unlocked!

You push it open, and pull Liz inside the warm building. There's a staircase in front of you. You turn back and see the Strangler reaching the walkway leading up to the door. You have only seconds left before he'll get to you.

You and Liz race up the stairs just steps ahead of the menacing man. He catches you by the hand. "Got you!" he growls.

"Let me go!" you cry, twisting your hand in his. Liz pulls at you as you pull at him. You scratch at his gripping hand with your free hand. Gobs of soft wax are stuck under your fingernails. He's wax just like all the others.

Wax, but alive, too!

Twist your hand free and turn to PAGE 129.

"Go for the thick ones!" you instruct Liz.

You and Liz grab the fraying ropes and start climbing. "Get them!" Dr. Wicked shouts. He's not going to let you get away.

"Pull!" you encourage Liz. "Faster!"

You notice a few strands of rope coming lose under your hands. Maybe we should have taken the other ropes, you think. But there's no time for that now. You've got to climb!

It's harder than you thought it would be. The ropes aren't anchored anywhere, so you and Liz swing wildly through the air.

What happens next is a total accident. You and Liz were just trying to get away, that's all. But while you are swinging out of control, you accidentally swing into Dr. Wicked. And Liz swings into the whole row of workers.

Like bowling pins being knocked over by a giant bowling ball, Dr. Wicked and the workers fall into the vats of hot wax below. Their screams fill the laboratory. Dr. Wicked is destroyed.

"It was them or us," you say to Liz as you slide down the ropes and land safely.

"Right," Liz says weakly. "Them or us."

"Mmfffffggbgbff!" a muffled voice says from the table.

Turn to PAGE 115.

Liz screams, too. And no wonder!

One of Sybil's eyes is blue. One is brown. The brown one is bigger than the blue one. And two inches higher on her face.

A puckered seam runs down the side of her nose. The seam continues around her mouth and runs off the edge of her jaw.

One cheek has freckles. The other doesn't. Her forehead has a tuft of hair growing out the middle of it. Red hair.

Sybil's face is like a patchwork quilt. Out of your worst nightmare!

"Stop screaming!" Sybil cries. "I know the horror of my face. I've seen it, too." She throws a purple-sleeved arm across her face and steps back, knocking against a rack of wax legs.

"I'm sorry," you start to say. "I didn't —"

"Save it," Sybil interrupts. "I don't have time to chat with you. I've got to get you to my new, improved Face Lifter!"

You and Liz both gasp. "You're going to lift our faces?" Liz squeaks.

"That's right." Sybil laughs. "I'm going to lift them — right off your skulls!"

Go to PAGE 127.

"Forget it, skull-face!" you say. "No way are we going to help you. Not after all you did to us! You got yourself into the Deboner. Now you can get yourself out."

"Aaaargh!" Axel howls with rage.

You and Liz walk away, leaving him hanging in the claws of the Deboner. You can hear him thrashing and trying to get loose. But you don't pay any attention to it.

That is, until a heavy hand falls on your shoulder.

"So you were just going to leave me there to be deboned like a piece of chicken," Axel growls in your ear.

Oh, no! He's free! Somehow he managed to escape the machine's awful claws!

You're terrified. But you have to ask.

"Wh-what are you going to do to us?" you croak.

Turn to PAGE 106.

You're out of the Parts Room at last! But Axel and Sybil are just behind you. And you've made them mad. REALLY mad.

You're now in a long hallway. Once again the walls are painted purple. "Boy, am I sick of purple!" you mutter.

"Yeah," Liz agrees. "If we ever get home again, I'm getting rid of every purple thing I own!"

There are no doors on this hallway. At the end, though, there are two identical stainless steel escalators. One goes up. The other goes down.

You rush to the foot of the down escalator and peer down. It's totally dark. You can't see where the escalator goes.

Liz investigates the up escalator. "I can't see a thing," she reports. "Which way should we go?"

"I'm not sure," you answer.

"There they are!" Sybil's voice echoes down the hall.

You've got to choose now. Up or down?

If you're not wearing a hat, go up to PAGE 84.
If you are wearing a hat, go down to PAGE 61.

"Down will take us deeper underground," you reason. "Let's go up."

You and Liz hop onto the escalator. It carries you swiftly upward. After a moment, you glance over your shoulder.

Sybil and Axel are at the foot of the escalator! Axel is peering up. You press deeper into the shadows. Can he see you?

"They're down there," you whisper to Liz.

"I can't believe this is happening to us," Liz whispers. "I can't believe Sybil wants to lift our faces!"

The escalator reaches the top. You step off and find yourselves in front of a purple velvet curtain. A sign next to it says DO NOT DISTURB. From behind the curtain comes a faint buzzing noise. Like a distant swarm of bees.

Then the sound of voices drifts to you from the escalator. "If they come this way, they're ours. Warm up the Face Lifter, Axel!" Sybil is commanding.

"It's them!" Liz says in a panic. "We've got to move!"

Ordinarily, you would obey a sign that said DO NOT DISTURB. But this is no ordinary situation.

You and Liz duck under the curtain.

Turn to PAGE 39.

"I'm going to wake one up," you say. "I bet she can give us advice on getting out of here."

Bending down, you take Sybil 85 by the shoulders. Her skin feels cold and gooey. Yuck! But this is no time to be squeamish! You shake her gently.

Nothing happens.

You shake again. Harder. Still nothing. "She's a heavy sleeper," you complain. "Liz, try one of the other ones."

Soon you and Liz are both shaking away. But the sleeping Sybils just keep snoring! What's wrong with them?

"Hah!" a voice behind you suddenly sneers. Axel! "You've fallen right into Miss Sybil's wax trap!"

Wax trap?

You spin around. That is, you try to. But you can't. Your hands are stuck fast in Sybil 85's gooey skin!

Turn to PAGE 123 if you can.

You lean closer to the Executioner.

This time you're sure. The wax figure's chest is definitely moving. Slowly. In and out. Is this part of the exhibit?

"What are you doing?" Liz jokes. "Checking him for bad breath?"

"Do you see it?" you whisper.

"See what?" Liz asks. She takes a closer look at the wax ax-man. Then her eyes grow wide. "They made it look like he's breathing!"

The spotlight above the exhibit flickers. Liz grabs your arm. "This is too creepy," she cries. "Let's find Jake and get out of here."

But you're too busy examining the Executioner. Curiosity overcomes fear. You scratch at one waxy hand with your fingernail. It kind of grosses you out, but at the same time, it fascinates you.

All the while, the big wax figure's barrel chest moves in and out — ever so gently.

Turn to PAGE 78 to see what you find.

At exactly the same moment, all the Sybils open their almost-identical mouths and shriek. "EEEEEEEEEE!"

Then, like an army of zombies, they climb off their shelves and start toward you.

"Run!" you yell to Liz.

"That word is getting really annoying," Liz pants as you tear toward the far end of the huge room.

She's right. If you get out of this nightmare, you're going out for track. After all this practice, you'll be a star!

Except that it's starting to seem like you won't get out. You can see the wall now. But you don't see any doors.

The zombie Sybils are closing in! You gaze around. There's nowhere else to run — except back through the Sybils.

You realize you're still carrying the object you knocked off the shelf. What is it? You look down at it.

Hey! It's a blowtorch!

If you try to run through the Sybils, turn to PAGE 19.

If you decide to use the blowtorch, turn to PAGE 68.

All at once the living, breathing wax villains step, crawl, and fall out of their horror scenes. Clawed hands, fanged mouths, and slime-covered arms reach out for you and Liz.

You decide not to stick around and find out what they have in mind. "Run, Liz!" you cry over the shouts, moans, and groans of the pack of creatures. "Run to the Skin Center!"

You both make a mad dash for the end of the hall.

But Count Dracula is a step ahead of you! His cold, waxy form steps into your path just before you get to the glass door. He smiles a horrible, fanged smile.

You put on the brakes and take a step back.

The rest of the wax attackers line up behind the Count. The Wolfman howls. The Frankenstein monster groans. Breathing their hot, rancid breath in your faces, they advance on you.

You retreat in sheer terror. Your legs are shaking. Liz's teeth are chattering.

Looks as if they've got you trapped. The door behind you is locked! Remember?

Dracula licks his lips hungrily. . . .

With all these monsters breathing down your necks, there's only one thing you can think of to do.

Go to PAGE 55.

"Yeow! He's a monster!" Liz yells.

"Wh-what happened to your face?" you croak.

Axel clacks his yellow teeth together. "Don't you like it? My boss, Sybil Wicked, gave me a face-lift."

Huh? "A face-lift?" you repeat, horrified.

"His boss?" Liz whispers.

You stare at each other. You just had a horrible idea.

"Um — where are you taking us, Axel?" you ask.

"To Miss Sybil, of course," Axel says. "I faxed pictures of your faces on ahead to her. She's *dying* to meet you both."

You gulp. You don't know who this Miss Sybil is, or what she wants with you, but you don't feel any need to find out. You've got to get out of this limo!

"The phone!" Liz whispers in your ear. "Call 911!"

Great idea! You reach for the phone. That's when you notice it has only three buttons. And none of them says 911.

One button has a picture of a clock on it. The second has a laughing jester's face. The third is completely blank.

You've got to push one of them. It's your only chance. But which one?

If you try the button with the clock, turn to PAGE 22.

If you try the blank button, turn to PAGE 35.

If you try the laughing jester, turn to PAGE 72.

"Bed," you decide. "The doors are too risky."

You and Liz dive under the bed. It's a tight fit. The springs sag, making it hard to move. And the dust is so thick you figure it hasn't been cleaned since the last ice age!

Next to you, Liz makes a strangled sound. She must be trying not to sneeze, you think.

"Shhh!" you hush her.

You hear a door opening, though you can't tell which one. The footsteps are in the room now. You hold your breath.

Liz's arm is smushed up against your face. It feels kind of . . . wet. Gross! You reach out to shove her away.

Your hand sinks into something slimy. Something that pulses gently. Something that's making a gurgling sound, so quietly that only you can hear it.

Something that *isn't* Liz!

Turn to PAGE 128.

"Footsteps!" you say to Liz. After your brush with the evil Executioner, you're not taking any chances. "Quick, let's hide!"

You search for a place to hide, but the room is empty! Except for one thing. So you do the only thing you can . . .

You duck under the dead Executioner's black cape.

A moment later you hear a man's voice. "I told those kids to wait in the lobby!" he says angrily. "Now they're holding up the whole group!"

It's Mr. Dunning!

"Mr. Dunning!" Liz calls out as you throw off the cape. "It's us! We're here!"

But he's not there. Where could he have gone? you wonder.

Then, through a small doorway you hadn't noticed before, you hear his voice again: "I told those kids to wait in the lobby!"

"Mr. Dunning!" you shout. And the two of you burst through the little doorway into . . . a closet!

What's going on? you think. Then you see something that makes your blood run cold.

Quick! Go to PAGE 77!

"Tip the stretcher over!" you call out to Jake. "Lean!"

But the noise of the sparks and short circuits makes it impossible for Jake to hear you. He's a prisoner of the stretcher and it's taking him to the next step — the final step.

The Skin Scraping Center is alive with workers scrambling to steady themselves and save the equipment. "Come on, Liz," you say breathlessly. "After Jake!"

"Oh," Liz cries hopelessly. "The end is near. I just know this is going to be it for us. For all of us."

Hurry to Page 124.

Someone is watching you! You feel it. There's something in the shadows across the room. And you have to find out what it is!

Maybe it's Jake! you think. Maybe this whole thing is one of his pranks. Maybe he put his sneakers on that conveyor belt so you'd *think* he was unconscious.

Maybe not.

"Jake?" you call hopefully. "Is that you?"

There's no reply.

"Mr. Dunning?" you try again.

A spotlight suddenly shines down from the ceiling. It blinds you for a moment. Then you and Liz both gasp.

The light is shining on a person, but it sure isn't Mr. Dunning. This giant wears a black hood and black cape. He holds a gleaming ax blade high in the air. In a moment he will bring it down on the victim kneeling before him.

"It's the Executioner!" you exclaim, horrified. "He was in one of the GOOSEBUMPS books we read, remember, Liz?"

"Yeah," Liz whispers. "The Executioner." Her eyes are wide. She can hardly breathe.

Then she screams. "It's Jake! He's going to be executed!"

Turn to PAGE 99.

The tall, shadowy figure of a man stands in a swirling cloud of mist. He wears a dark overcoat and a wide-brimmed hat pulled down over his eyes. As the fog clears you see that his hands are stretched out in front of him. He's reaching for Liz's throat.

"Look out! He's going to strangle you!" you exclaim.

Liz ducks. The Strangler keeps reaching for her. This time you reach for her, too. You pull her in the opposite direction and start running.

Are those footsteps behind you? Is the Strangler following you? You desperately want to look back. But it might slow you down.

If you look back over your shoulder, turn to PAGE 50.

If you keep running and don't look back, turn to PAGE 8.

Liz is staring at a framed, yellowed newspaper clipping that hangs on the wall. "It's about a terrible fire at Dr. Wicked's lab, three years ago," she whispers. She points at a photo. "That was his daughter. He was teaching her his secret method for making lifelike wax dummies."

You lean forward and peer at the photo. It shows a girl with long black hair. Her face has been cut out of the picture. "'Sybil Wicked, age 14, was lost in the blaze,'" you read.

You feel very cold all of a sudden. "Liz," you say. "Didn't Axel say he works for Sybil Wicked?"

Liz nods. Her freckled face is pale.

"But how?" you ask. "How can he work for someone who's . . . dead?"

Go to PAGE 73.

How a-MAZE-ing are you? Start at the THIS WAY OUT sign. As you follow your chosen path, collect the letters along the way. Write them in the space provided here. If you have chosen the correct path, your letters will spell out an important message from the owner of the Wicked Wax Museum, Dr. Wicked himself!

Write the letters here in the order in which you find them:

___ ___ ___ ___   ___ ___ ___   ___ ___ ___

___ ___ ___ ___   ___ ___ ___ ___

If you finish the maze successfully, go straight to PAGE 124. If you don't get through the maze, close the book and take a cold shower. You've just been riding on a river of burning wax!

"Aaaaaahhhh!" you yell. Your voice trails away behind you as you plummet down. Down. Down.

SPLAT! You land on something soft. And squishy. And smelly.

"Peee-yew!" Liz's voice complains next to you.

"Liz!" you cry. You struggle to sit up. "What happened? Where are we?"

"In the garbage," Liz tells you.

You gaze around. You're surrounded by mounds of banana peels, coffee grounds, chicken bones, and rotting vegetables. Giant, buzzing flies swarm around your heads. Yecch! You must have fallen through a trap door right into a Dumpster.

With a jerk, the Dumpster starts to move. Liz peers over the side. "We're on some kind of train track," she reports. "And we're headed for that dark tunnel up ahead."

Dark tunnel? "Maybe we should get off now," you suggest. Then you think again. "Or maybe we should stay put. This Dumpster could be our ticket out of here!"

If you decide to stay put, turn to PAGE 29.

If you decide to get out now, turn to PAGE 76.

"What do you mean, skin Jake alive?" Liz cries.

"Remember one of the masked guys talked about getting Jake ready for the 'next step'?" you ask. "Jake got through the steaming step. The sign above the end of the tunnel says Skin Scraping Center. That must be the next step!"

"You mean they're going to scrape Jake's skin . . . off?" Liz shudders. "But why?"

"I haven't figured that out yet," you admit. "But I know we've got to save him. Quick, get back into your test tube!"

"WHAT?" Liz cries. "Are you crazy?"

"Trust me," you say. "It's the only way to follow Jake!"

You push Liz back into her tube. Then you jump into your own tube and pull the door closed.

Just as you hoped, the track starts moving again. You and Liz are headed for the Skin Scraping Center!

You hope you won't be too late to save Jake. That is, if you can survive yourselves. . . .

Hurry to PAGE 26.

Your stomach turns over. Liz is right! The figure kneeling with his head on the chopping block has chin-length brown hair — just like Jake's!

"Jake!" you shriek. You dash over and grab his hand to pull him off the chopping block. But what you feel startles you. Jake's hand is covered with wax!

Right then the Executioner's arms glide downward. The ax gleams in the spotlight.

WHACK! The steel ax blade lands squarely on Jake's neck!

Quick, turn to PAGE 42!

100

It's Mr. Dunning! The rest of your class is standing behind him. Everyone is staring at you.

"I thought I told you to stay inside!" he yells. "This is the last straw. You've had it this time."

"But I — but —" you sputter.

"No buts," Mr. Dunning orders. "I'm calling your parents right now!" And he marches back to the lobby.

The kids from your class are still there, staring at you. "What a loser," someone mutters. A couple of them start to snicker. You feel about two inches tall.

Looks like you made the wrong choice in . . .

THE END

"I have to know what's going on," you tell Liz. You turn in the direction of the voice and cry, "Who are you?"

"I'm Sybil Wicked," says the voice. "Dr. Wicked's daughter."

"But the newspaper clipping!" Liz protests. "It said you were lost in a fire!"

"Yes," the voice agrees softly. "I was lost. But not in the way you think. Not in the way the world thinks!"

"Wh-what do you mean?" you quaver.

In answer, Sybil Wicked moves slowly out from the shadows.

First you see her hands. They're small, delicate. Next, her arms and body. She is wearing a long, purple robe. Like the ones in the closet.

At last her head comes into the light. Long, beautiful black hair hides her face as she gazes at the ground.

Then she looks up. And you can't hold back a scream.

Turn to PAGE 81.

You've got a feeling there's more to that closet than meets the eye. . . .

"Come on," you urge Liz. "I think we should go back into the closet. I think it's the way out."

This time you lead the way into the closet. You push aside masses of those strange, identical purple robes. And then you spot the thing you were searching for.

At the back of the closet is a revolving door! You knew it! "Whee!" you shout as you whirl on through. But when you come out the other side, your cry dies in your throat.

"Ugh!" Liz mutters.

You couldn't agree more. You've never seen a more horrifying place in your life!

Swallow hard and go to PAGE 125.

You stare at the lifeline in your palm. It barely reaches past the middle of your palm.

That's funny, you think. I could have sworn it used to be longer!

Meanwhile, you're spinning out of control. You feel like a piece of taffy — all twisted, pulled, and stretched to the limit. You feel suddenly soft and waxy.

"I feel like a licorice Twizzler!" you cry from the funnel.

"Well, I feel like . . ." Before Liz can say what she feels like, the tornado drops you down in a soft, sticky mountain of marshmallow cream. You're on top of a cake! Next to you are long twisted things sticking into the marshmallow cream. And these things have wicks sticking out of their tops.

Now you both know exactly what you feel like. You feel like twisted wax candles on a birthday cake!

And that's exactly what you are. Dr. Wicked's most brilliant invention is this twisting tornado waxer. Victims caught in the funnel turn to wax. What a strange twist of fate. Your future in the wax museum is as candles burning on the grand opening celebration cake. It will be the beginning for the Wicked Wax Museum. But for you and Liz it will be . . .

THE END

"It's Jake!" Liz exclaims aloud.

Both the worker and Dr. Wicked swing around to see who spoke. They see you and Liz.

"After them!" Dr. Wicked orders. "After them!"

"Run!" you shout. "Run for your life!"

With all the workers in the laboratory coming after you, there's only one way out of this: up.

Your thoughts are racing as fast as your feet. You've got it! You could climb the scaffolding on those ropes. Then you could swing down and tackle Dr. Wicked.

It's risky. No, it's more than risky. It's life-threatening. But you have no choice other than which ropes to climb. You examine them closely. Some look too thin to support your weight. Others are thicker—but starting to fray. Which one will you choose?

If you go for a thin rope, turn to PAGE 71.

If you go for a thick, fraying rope, turn to PAGE 80.

The cries come from behind the left-hand purple door — the one you didn't go through. Axel shakes his bony head. "Better see what's wrong," he mutters to himself.

Bending close to you, he clacks his teeth together. "Don't go anywhere," he warns. "I'd sure hate for you to miss the fun!" Then he hurries through the left-hand door.

Fun! Hah! You don't waste a second. The minute he's gone you fling the rope off your wrists. Then you get to work on Liz.

"Hurry!" she urges. "He'll be back any second!"

You pick frantically at the knotted ropes. You can hear Axel's voice through the door. "Sorry, Miss Sybil," he says. "I thought I took all the mirrors away."

"The horror!" the wailing voice cries again.

At last the knots give. "Let's get out of here," you say.

"I think there's a hall that way," Liz says, pointing at the door Axel just went through. "Should we check it out?"

Should you try the left-hand door? Or should you go back and finish exploring the closet?

To explore the closet, turn to PAGE 102.
To try the left-hand door, turn to PAGE 74.

Axel hoists you up by your shirt collar. In the other hand, he's got Liz. You both kick and struggle, but it does no good. Axel is inhumanly strong! His bony jaws clack as he laughs his demented laugh.

"I should take you to Miss Sybil," he tells you. "But I don't want to. I can always get her more victims. And you two have made me very angry. I want to punish you."

He hauls you over to the Deboner. "Let's see how you like this," he chuckles, and tosses you into the funnel. Mechanical claws swoop down instantly and seize you. In less than ten seconds, you're hanging like clothes on a line. A tiny jigsaw whirs directly toward your eyes. You hear Liz scream.

Turn to PAGE 134.

You pound on the glass, fighting to escape. A sudden rush of steam whooshes in through a hose in the top of the tube.

You can't breathe! Sweat drips down your forehead. Your fingernails scrape across the glass as you claw at the door. The steam is getting thicker and there's no way out!

"I'm suffocating!" You choke out the words. "Let me out!"

You beat the glass with your fists, but your hands are limp and useless. The steam has softened them too much. You're shriveling like a prune. This steaming process is shrinking you. You're the size of a Barbie doll!

"Help!" you cry. Even your voice is smaller now. The two men in doctor's masks can't hear you. They glance at your test tube and shake their heads. "Another goner!" says one man, matter-of-factly. "I guess this one couldn't take the heat."

You feel a little sick. A little tired. A little little. When they open the door, you're just a speck on the bottom of the test tube. The good news is, your steaming is finished.

The bad news is, so are you.

THE END

You decide to push the laughing jester button once more. And this time, the phone on the other end rings.

And rings.

And rings.

And rings.

You're about to slam the receiver down when someone answers.

"Hello?" you scream into the mouthpiece. "Hello?"

"May I be of some assistance?" a man's voice asks.

You know that voice. You jerk your head up and see Axel holding a phone to the earhole of his bony head. He's laughing and laughing and laughing.

You stare at the laughing jester on the phone button. How could you have thought it looked friendly? How come you didn't notice before that the jester's face is a skull?

Looks like the joke's on you!

THE END

You and Liz waste no time getting out of there. Back down on the street, you gaze up at the building. From the window at the very top, the museum worker sticks his head out and screams, "You'll pay for this! You'll pay! We've got your friend Jake, and we'll get you, too!"

"Hurry, Liz," you say. "We better get out of here."

She's groaning and rubbing her ankle. "I can't run anymore," she says. "My ankle's too sore. I need to rest a minute."

You gaze up the street and see the man in overalls coming out of the building he was in.

Quickly, you pull Liz into the dark doorway of the nearest building. By mistake, she leans back against the door and hits the doorbell.

BZZZZZZ! An ear-stinging buzzer sounds.

The door opens automatically. A long hallway stretches in front of you. At the end of it a woman motions to you to come in. It's the ticket lady from the lobby of the museum. What's she doing here? you wonder. Uh-oh. Something's fishy.

If you turn back, turn to PAGE 43.
If you go inside, turn to PAGE 116.

110

After a while you decide it's safe to open your eyes again.

Hey, who turned out the lights? You can't see a thing!

"Hello?" you try to call.

There's something wrong. You can't seem to open your mouth to form the words!

An awful suspicion is forming in your mind. With trembling fingers, you reach up to touch your face.

There's nothing there! No eyes, no mouth, no nose. Instead, all you feel is blank, smooth wax.

"No! No! No!" you moan. Or you try to moan. Actually, it sounds more like, "Mmm! Mmm! Mmm!" because you have no mouth.

You don't want to believe it. But she did it. Sybil Wicked really did it. She stole your face.

Face it! This is really . . .

THE END

You're beginning to believe Jake's screams really aren't a joke. Still, you don't want to go through the pitch-dark doorway that yawns in front of you. "We'd better ask someone for help," you suggest.

You look around the lobby. "There's no one here except that weird ticket lady," Liz whispers. "She looks like a fortune-teller in that purple turban. She gives me the creeps."

"Well, creepy or not, she's the only one here," you point out. You approach the ticket window. The ticket lady is sitting with her back to you. "Excuse me," you say.

The ticket lady doesn't speak or move.

"Excuse me," you say a little louder. "We think our friend is in trouble. Can you help us?"

Still no answer.

"Why won't you answer?" Liz yells. "What's wrong with you?"

"Maybe she's deaf," you whisper. You reach into the booth to tap the ticket lady on the arm.

Her arm is cold and hard. You gasp. "She's not real! She's only a wax figure! What's going on here?"

Turn to PAGE 12.

What was that awful racket? You spin around.

Oh, no! Liz has stumbled and banged into the purple door! Her watch clacks against the painted wood.

"What was that?" a female voice demands sharply. "Axel, go see. If those kids are trying to escape, bring them to me. I'll make short work of them!"

You don't wait to hear any more. "In here!" you whisper. You and Liz rush through the yellow door and slam it behind you. It's darker than midnight inside. But your groping fingers find a key in the keyhole. You turn it. Safe!

And not a moment too soon! Axel pounds on the other side of the door. "Come out of there, my little friends," he yells. "Come out at once, or you'll be very sorry!"

"In your dreams!" you retort. "Liz, see if you can find a light switch. Then we'll find a way out of here!"

"Here it is," Liz announces. She flips the switch.

Oh, boy, do you wish she hadn't done that.

To find out why, go to PAGE 53.

"Sure I'm sure he's wax," you laugh. "Look. I'll prove it. I'll put my neck right in his hands, see?" You back up to the wax figure and slide your neck between his outstretched hands. For once, one of these wax figures really *is* just wax. To convince Liz, you stand this way for a few seconds. "Look," you joke. "He's strangling me! Ha-ha! Help!"

"Very funny," Liz says.

"Okay, okay," you say, giving up the joke. "He's not really strangling me. Who would want to strangle a nice kid like me?"

You start to step forward out of the Strangler's hands. Warm fingers tighten around your neck. You feel your air being cut off. You can't scream or talk or breathe. Mist surrounds you again. You feel as if you're floating. You can't see a thing. Everything is dark.

Everything is nothing now.

Who would want to strangle a nice kid like you?

The Strangler would, that's who.

THE END

Spider webs? No thanks! "Let's try to climb out," you suggest quickly.

"Yeah. At least we know that chute goes back up to the road. Give me a boost, will you?" Liz asks.

You boost her up to the mouth of the chute. She finds a handhold and hauls herself into the darkness.

A moment later her hand reaches out and clasps yours. Huffing and puffing, she pulls you up until you can grab some handholds yourself.

You pull yourself into the chute and peer ahead. The chute looks as if it goes almost straight up! "I don't know if we can do this," you pant.

In answer, Liz points down. You look where she's pointing. A hideous skull-face is grinning up at you from the stone cell. Axel! How did he get down there? you wonder. His hands are reaching for you . . . only inches from your ankles!

"Go, go, go!" you yell, pushing Liz from behind as you scramble frantically up the chute.

Scramble to PAGE 121.

"Jake!" you and Liz exclaim together. But this time you call out his name with happiness instead of horror.

You hurry over to the table he's tied to, and pull the tape off his mouth and eyes.

"What do you think, Liz?" you ask, winking at her. "Should we unstrap him? After all, he's the one who got us into this mess in the first place."

"Come on," Jake pleads. "This was no picnic for me either, you know. They had me heading for the bath of the century."

You and Liz laugh as you untie Jake. He stands up, shakes his legs to get the circulation going, and says, "So, what did I miss?"

Liz rolls her eyes. You're just about to give Jake a friendly punch on the shoulder, when you hear another familiar voice.

"Uh-oh," you say. "Here comes more trouble."

Turn to PAGE 65.

You go inside the building and slam the door behind you.

Once inside you see a lighted sign on the wall. It flashes: black, red, black, red. When it flashes red, the word FUTURE is spelled out in black. When it flashes black, the word PAST is spelled out in red.

The woman who was selling tickets in the lobby stares into a crystal ball. She's really a fortuneteller! Well, that explains that wacky purple turban she's wearing.

As you approach her she looks up at you. "I know all from my crystal ball," she says mysteriously. "I see you are the ones with no tickets, eh? And how will you pay your way?"

"W-well," you stammer. "I mean we don't have any money on us or anything. Mr. Dunning was supposed to . . ."

"It's too late for tickets now. You're already in. What you need is a ticket out!" She swirls her hands over the crystal ball and asks you to make your choice. "Red or black? Future or past? You must decide, and you must decide fast!"

It's too hard to decide on your own. Let a deck of cards help you. Go find a pack in your house and pick a card.

If you pick a red card for FUTURE, turn to PAGE 23.

If you pick a black card for PAST, turn to PAGE 1.

You flip the switch! The Suction Screen lets you go. You jump to the side, out of its range. "Run, Liz!" you shout.

At the sound of your voice, Axel and Sybil look up. "Axel, they're getting away! After them!" Sybil cries.

Liz darts behind some shelves. You stand your ground next to the Suction Screen. "Come and get me!" you shout.

Axel runs toward you. You wait, hoping your plan works. Your hand hovers over the giant purple switch. He comes closer. . . . Closer . . .

"Now!" you cry, and flip the switch to ON.

ZOOP! Axel is instantly sucked against the lavender screen. He's trapped! Now all you have to worry about is Sybil.

You turn to face her. But when you see what's happening to her, your eyes bug out.

She's falling apart. Literally! She got a little too close to the Suction Screen. And it's ripping great hunks of flesh right off her face! They fly through the air and thud against the screen. "NO!" Sybil shrieks.

You feel sick. Sybil's old, patchwork face was hideous enough. But what's underneath is truly terrifying.

Go to PAGE 56 if you dare!

So what if your parents told you not to get in strange cars? This is an exception! "All right!" you exclaim.

Liz steps into the luxurious limo first and leans back in the buttery leather seat. You follow her in and reach for a soda.

Without warning, the door slams. Power locks click. Seat belts shoot out and strap you tightly in place. Strapped — and trapped! Axel guns the engine.

"Hey!" you yell. "What's going on?"

The limo roars away. You twist in your seat to stare back at the museum. Where's Mr. Dunning when you need him?

A figure runs out the front door. "It's Jake!" Liz cries.

Jake is waving his arms and shouting. You can hear his words faintly. "Come back!" he yells. "It was just a joke!"

"A joke?" Liz sputters. "I'm going to kill Jake."

A sudden burst of blue light, like a camera flash, blinds you. When you can see again, you glare at Axel in the rearview mirror. "What's the big idea?" you ask.

Or you start to ask. Actually, the words never leave your mouth. Instead, you gape in horror at Axel's face.

Rattle on to PAGE 89.

He has a square jaw, you notice. You can see its shape clearly. Very clearly. Because there's no skin covering it.

Axel's face is a bare skull!

What are you, nuts?

Of course it's a real emergency! No, don't argue. Get over to PAGE 36 and break that glass RIGHT NOW!

Race to PAGE 36.

You panic.

"AAHHHH!" you scream. "THE WAX FIGURE IS ALIVE!"

You have good reason to panic, too. You peeled a little wax off his hand. Now all the wax is flaking off his body — like skin peeling after a bad sunburn. You try to pull yourself away from his waxy grip, but he's too strong.

"Liz! HELP!" you cry, turning your head to look for her. But Liz has troubles of her own.

Her red curly hair is completely tangled in an air vent on the wall. The more she struggles, the tighter the tangles become. She gazes at you, wide-eyed.

Looks as if you're on your own against the Executioner. He's holding you with one hand. With the other, he raises his gleaming steel ax. . . .

If you're right-handed, go to PAGE 70.
If you're left-handed, go to PAGE 63.

Taking two steps up, sliding one step back, you make the long climb. Liz slips. You slip. You pick yourselves up and go on.

All the while, the hair on the back of your neck is standing straight up. Is Axel behind you? Are his fingers about to clamp around your ankle?

Suddenly Liz breaks the silence with a joyful shout.

"We're here!" she exclaims gleefully. "We made it back!"

You look past Liz. "Hey!" you cry. "We're back in the museum!"

Sure enough, you've popped out in the lobby in front of the Wicked Wax Museum. In front of you is a familiar red door. It's wide open. Open into darkness.

"Aaaaaauurghhhh! Help!" A long, choking scream comes out of the dark. You and Liz grin at each other.

"Nice try, Jake," you yell. "But we know it's just a joke."

"NO!" Jake's voice sounds so terrified you start to wonder. "Not this time! HELP ME!"

Then there's a thud. Then silence. Then a motor starts up.

You stare at Liz and wonder if your face is as pale as hers.

"I think it's for real," she whispers.

Turn to PAGE 30.

There's no safe place to go. The door behind you is locked. The door ahead of you leads to skin scraping — whatever that is.

But you know you have to get there and save Jake. You and Liz cling to each other as you walk through the Hall of Horrors. Past Count Dracula. Past the Creature from the Black Lagoon. Past the Mud Monsters. Past all of them.

The hall is about as long as a football field. And about halfway through, you stop. Did you see what you thought you saw?

You study the waxy red drops of blood clinging to Dracula's fangs. His lips are curled back, showing blood-soaked gums and a crimson tongue. Out of the corner of your eye, you see the scaly Creature from the Black Lagoon in the next exhibit case. His webbed hands clutch the long hair of his victim.

And tighten their grip in front of your eyes!

You weren't just imagining things! Count Dracula really is turning to focus his red eyes on you. And so are all the figures in this wicked hall of wax.

They're all alive! Just like the Executioner!

As if they can read your thoughts, suddenly all the wax creatures drop their victims and turn their evil eyes on YOU!

Race to PAGE 88!

These sleeping Sybils are made of wax! And the wax has melted and swallowed your hands!

"Don't bother to struggle," Axel says cheerfully. "This is very special wax. You can't break free."

You try anyway, of course. But Axel's right.

You're trapped!

"Miss Sybil," Axel calls. "We've got them."

"Excellent," a female voice answers. "Just give me a moment to prepare the Face Lifter."

The Face Lifter! You and Liz exchange horrified glances.

"NOOO!" you shout, and strain more frantically than ever to pull your hands free. In fact, you struggle so hard you begin to hyperventilate. Suddenly the room is swimming in front of your eyes. And then you faint.

Turn to PAGE 17.

Uh-oh. It looks like your end might be here. Yours. And Liz's. And Jake's. You're in the Wax Dipping Laboratory, and it's very clear now what is going on at this Wicked Wax Museum.

You look around for Jake and spy an empty stretcher. But no Jake. Huge vats of hot bubbling wax are lined up across the center of the lab. Dozens of ropes hang from scaffolding. Giant machines rumble, tumble, swish, and swirl. Hundreds of wax-dipped figures dangle from drying racks. A voice on the other side of the laboratory shouts, "Check that one for readiness!"

"Yes, Dr. Wicked," replies a worker in white.

Now you see him. It's Dr. Izzy Wicked himself standing on a platform overlooking the lab. A mane of wild white hair frames his hollow-cheeked face. "Don't dip him until you're sure the steaming and skinning has been successful!" he orders.

Three other workers are gathered around a stainless steel table. When they step back you see what — or who — they're examining. It's Jake!

Go to PAGE 104.

You're in a huge, shadowy room full of wheeled clothes racks. But instead of clothes, the racks are hung with hundreds of wax body parts. Pale, waxy arms and legs dangle before you. Ears, noses, and eyeballs are strung on clotheslines like a string of holiday ornaments.

A sudden breeze sighs through the room. You back away from a swinging arm — and step into a curtain of ears. Gross!

You can't tell if there's a way out at the other end of the room. But you know you can't go back. So you and Liz pick your way between the racks. You're trying hard not to panic. Then Liz taps you on the shoulder. "Look at this."

You see an empty rack. A note is taped to it. You read:

"New Parts. Due Today."

An eerie voice speaks from the shadows behind you. "You're right on time. I've been expecting you."

Yikes! "Wh-who's there?" you stammer, starting to turn.

Liz grips your arm. "We don't need to know! Let's ride this empty rack like a skateboard and get out of here — fast!"

If you jump onto the rack, turn to PAGE 20.
If you turn to see who spoke, turn to PAGE 101.

You stare at your palm. You don't have a clue which line on your hand is your lifeline.

"I don't think I can take this turning much longer," Liz moans. "I feel like I'm stuck in a blender!"

It's quieter in the eye of the tornado. So you don't have any trouble hearing her.

"Me, too," you say as the wind whips you around and around. "I just want to find Jake and get out of here."

The tornado funnel carries you up higher and higher. The next time you glance down, you see huge vats of swirling, bubbling, boiling liquid.

Men in white overalls are everywhere. Some are busy mixing. Some are measuring. And some are stirring whatever is in those vats. A strong odor rises up and reaches your nose.

You know exactly what the smell is. Hot wax!

Go to PAGE 67.

Sybil continues in her cold voice, "I've experimented with many face-replacement techniques. My new one requires a whole face. I'll use one of you to test it. The other will become the new face of Sybil Wicked. And then I'll reveal myself to the world, and show them that my brilliance has not died! I'm holding a press conference later today."

You and Liz stare at each other. "She's batty," you say.

"True," Liz agrees. "There's only one thing to do."

You nod. "Here we go again. RUN!"

The two of you take off. Behind you, Sybil screams with rage. "Axel! Get them!" she shouts.

Pounding footsteps tell you the skull-faced driver is close on your heels. You crash through racks of waxy arms, legs, torsos. *Where's the exit?* you wonder frantically.

There doesn't seem to be one. Instead, you and Liz find yourselves in a corner. There's nowhere to go. You're trapped!

Axel and Sybil are standing there, laughing at you. This is it. You're done for.

Or . . . are you? You spot a glass box on the wall. Letters on the box say:

IN CASE OF EMERGENCY, BREAK GLASS.

If you think this is an emergency, turn to PAGE 36.

If you don't think it's a real emergency, turn to PAGE 119.

There really *are* monsters under the bed!

You want to scream in terror. But you can't, because then whoever is in the room will hear you. So you battle the slimy thing under the bed in silence. Kicking. Shoving. Even biting.

The trouble is, the more you struggle, the more the sticky goo gums up your hands, your face, every part of you.

Soon your mouth and eyes are sealed shut with the goo. You think it might be wise to yell now. But it's too late. You can't yell. You can't even move. You can only lie there, helpless, as the slime monster wraps itself around you and starts digesting you whole.

Oh, well . . . easy come, easy goo!

THE END

You twist and scratch until you pull yourself free from the wax madman. You grab Liz and pull her up the stairs. You reach the room where the light is on. There's no time to knock. You throw open the door —

— and come face-to-face with the tall museum worker who captured you in the Executioner's room. He's still wearing his white overalls, but he's taken off the doctor's mask.

"I've been expecting you," he says. "You didn't really think you could get away, did you? You're staying with us forever." He looks past you and speaks to the man behind you. "Aren't they, Strangler?"

You turn to run, but the Strangler's towering figure blocks the way.

"Why try to leave?" the man in overalls snarls. "You should feel honored to be part of the grand opening of the museum."

While he talks, you search the room with your eyes. You're looking for anything that might save you and Liz. Then you see it. The candle in the window.

You've got an idea! And it just might work.

You have no choice but to try it. Turn to PAGE 7.

"History!" The tall worker laughs. "That's a good one! The public wants horror, not history. And we aim to please. You've already met the Executioner. Soon you'll meet the others."

"Others?" you cry. "What others?"

The short man answers. "First things first. There's no time to steam you. We'll send you straight to the next step."

He pulls a red curtain aside. A door in the wall slides open to a dimly-lit hallway. At the far end there's a glass door with red letters on it. They say SKIN SCRAPING CENTER. And there's Jake on the other side!

"Jake!" you cry. "Hold on! We're coming to get you!" He's struggling in the arms of another masked museum worker. Now he's being strapped onto a rolling stretcher and pushed out of sight. He's gone again. But at least you know he's still alive!

"Get moving!" the tall man orders. They push you and Liz through the doorway. The door slides shut behind you and locks.

You and Liz are alone. Now's the time to make your move. You've got to act — before they turn Jake into a statue!

On the wall, two buttons glow. One is yellow. One is green. They look important. Just what you need to create a distraction. But which button should you push? Yellow? Or green?

If you push the yellow button, turn to PAGE 16.
If you push the green button, turn to PAGE 55.

"That's plain creepy!" Liz cries. "Stop the ride! I want to get off!"

She pushes hard against the metal lap bar. Everything screeches to a halt.

A moment later the lights go out. You're sitting in the dark again!

What happens next depends on what day of the week it is.

If you're reading this on a weekday, the ride starts right back up again. *Go to PAGE 51.*

If you're reading this on a weekend, you have to get off the ride. *Go to PAGE 25.*

You're so busy scratching the wax surface of the Executioner that you hardly notice what's happening. But it gradually dawns on you.

Fingers. Five of them. Fingers have wrapped themselves around your right arm. And they're starting to squeeze.

You can't bring yourself to raise your eyes to the Executioner's face. Your eyes are level with his chest. In and out. In and out.

You gulp. "Liz," you say. "I certainly hope that's *you* squeezing my arm."

"Knock it off," Liz says from across the room. "You're scaring me."

They're not Liz's fingers.

That can mean only one thing. . . .

What happens next depends on how easily scared you get. Are you the type who flies into a panic? Or are you cool and collected when things get scary?

Go ahead and test yourself. Hold out your hand away from your body. Can you keep your fingers perfectly still? Or do they wiggle and twitch?

If you can keep them still, go to PAGE 10.

If your fingers are trembling, even a little, go to PAGE 120.

The two men in doctor's masks drag you and Liz off the belt. "Two more for steaming," says one. "Dr. Wicked will be pleased."

They roughly load you and Liz into separate test tubes, close the glass doors, and seal them. "They're going to steam us!" your mind screams. "We'll die!"

Already you have to fight for breath. You've always been frightened of enclosed places. It's hard not to panic!

Your mind races, trying to come up with a plan. Now that you're away from the sleeping gas, you feel strength returning to your arms and legs. Maybe you can break out of this contraption! But what about the two men?

Besides, once the steaming starts — whatever it is — you'll probably need all the strength you can muster. Maybe you should lie low, try to conserve air and energy, and hope you come out alive. . . .

What'll it be?

If you fight to escape, go to PAGE 107.

If you stand perfectly still to save oxygen, go to PAGE 47.

The next thing you know, you're lying on the floor, staring up at a lavender ceiling. You feel all right. Kind of limp, but all right. "I think I'll get up and look around," you say to yourself.

But when you try to sit up, you get the shock of your life. Your body won't obey you. All you can do is ooze a little.

"What's happening?" you whimper. Out of the corner of your eye, you see a skin rug on the floor nearby. It's freckled. And it has a mop of red hair on top. And it's pulsing slowly.

With a shock, you realize it's Liz. Liz without her bones!

It's all coming back to you now. The Deboner machine. That's why you can't move. You've been deboned! You no longer have a skeleton! You're just an envelope of skin!

Make no bones about it, this is . . .

THE END

"I can't get in this car," you say reluctantly. "I'd get in big trouble with my parents."

"What?" Liz explodes. "Jake's in danger and all you can think about is what your parents will say? You wimp! Fine, stay there. I'm getting into the limo."

She climbs into the long black car. You stand on the pavement, feeling like an idiot. Then you hear her give a cry of surprise. "Jake!"

Huh? You bend down and peer into the car's interior. Sure enough, there's Jake, lounging on the buttery leather seat with his red sneakers propped on an embroidered footrest. He raises his soda can to you. "See you later, sucker," he calls.

"Wait! How did you get there?" you demand. But it's too late. The car door slams in your face. Dimly through the tinted window, you can see Liz and Jake inside. It looks as if they're laughing. Laughing at you, probably.

A deep, threatening voice behind you makes you spin around.

Spin to PAGE 100.

"I still think we should help Axel," you tell Liz. "No matter how awful he is, this horrible Deboner is worse!"

Liz looks doubtful. "All right," she says at last.

The drill is almost touching Axel's chest by now. You rush over and yank on the Deboner's electrical cord.

Sparks shoot from the outlet as the machine is unplugged. Slowly the drill stops turning. The claws drop Axel into the giant funnel. He picks himself up and climbs out.

"Thank you," he cries, hugging you and Liz. Tears pour down his bare cheekbones. "I'm so touched! No one's ever done anything nice for me before! You two are real friends."

"Great!" Liz grins. "So you'll let us go, right?"

Axel shakes his skull sadly. "I'm sorry," he says softly. "I can't do that. Miss Sybil would never forgive me."

Liz glares at you. "I knew I never should have listened to you!" she yells. "Come on, let's run!"

"Wait!" Axel cries.

Turn to PAGE 54.

About the Author

R.L. STINE is the most popular author in America. He is the creator of the *Goosebumps*, *Give Yourself Goosebumps*, *Fear Street*, and *Ghosts of Fear Street* series, among other popular books. He has written more than 100 scary novels for kids. Bob lives in New York City with his wife, Jane, teenage son, Matt, and dog, Nadine.

R.L. STINE
GIVE YOURSELF
Goosebumps®

This Evil Genie Has Got You in a Jam!

You and your brother are heading home from school. You grab a can of soda–and when you open it...a Genie pops out! Now you have three wishes. When you want to fly, she turns you into a vulture. When you want to be a famous star, she turns you into a TV monster. Now you have one wish left–and you're kind of wishing you were never born–but be careful, you-know-who can definitely arrange that!

What will you wish for? Choose from more than 20 spooky endings!

Give Yourself Goosebumps #13
Scream of the Evil Genie
by R.L. Stine

Coming soon to a bookstore near you!

Curly's All-New and Shocking
Goosebumps®
Fan Club Pack
Only $8.95
Plus $2.00 shipping and handling*
CURLY
Zipper tag
Glow-in-the-Dark Pen
Folder
Game sheets
Wallet
Shipping box
HERE LIES Goosebumps
THE OFFICIAL GOOSEBUMPS FAN CLUB
From the desk of
Notepad
Curly Bio
THE OFFICIAL Goosebumps FAN CLUB
CURLY
Unboo-lievable, dudes!
It's more exclusive, new Goosebumps stuff to collect!
Get the inside scary scoop on the latest books, the TV show, videos, games—and everything Goosebumps!
All this plus:
• Game sheets
• Notepad
• Sticker
• A subscription to the official newsletter, The Scream
(mailed separately—a few weeks after you receive your pack)
To get your all-new Goosebumps Fan Club Pack (in the U.S. and Canada only), just fill out the coupon below and send it with your check or money order. U.S. residents: $8.95 plus $2.00 shipping and handling to Goosebumps Fan Club, Scholastic Inc., P.O. Box 7500, 2931 East McCarty Street, Jefferson City, MO 65102. Canadian residents: $13.95 plus $2.00 shipping and handling to Goosebumps Fan Club, Scholastic Canada, 123 Newkirk Road, Richmond Hill, Ontario, L4C3G5. Offer expires 9/30/97. Offer good for one year from date of receipt. Please allow 4-6 weeks for your introductory pack to arrive.
*Canadian prices slightly higher. Fan club offer expires 9/30/97. Membership good for one year from date of receipt. Newsletters sent four times during membership.
Hurry! Send me my all-new Goosebumps Fan Club Pack. I am enclosing my check or money order (no cash please) for U.S. residents: $10.95 ($8.95 plus $2.00) and for Canadian residents: $15.95 ($13.95 plus $2.00).
Name________ Birthdate________
Address________
City________ State________ Zip________
Telephone (   )________ Boy________ Girl________
Where did you buy this book? ❑ Bookstore ❑ Book Fair ❑ Book Club ❑ Other
© 1996 Parachute Press, Inc. GOOSEBUMPS is a registered trademark of Parachute Press, Inc. All Rights Reserved.
GBFC396